MURDERERS
I HAVE KNOWN

Marina Warner's fiction includes *The Lost Father*
(Winner of a Commonwealth Writers' Prize and
shortlisted for the Booker Prize), *Indigo*, *The Leto
Bundle* and a previous collection of stories, *The
Mermaids in the Basement*. Her work on myth,
symbolism and fairy tale includes *Alone of All Her
Sex*, *From the Beast to the Blonde* and *No Go the
Bogeyman*.

ALSO BY MARINA WARNER

Fiction

In a Dark Wood

The Skating Party

The Lost Father

Wonder Tales (Editor)

The Mermaids in the Basement

Indigo

The Leto Bundle

Non-Fiction

The Dragon Empress

Alone of All Her Sex:
The Myth and the Cult of the Virgin Mary

Joan of Arc: The Image of Female Heroism

Monuments and Maidens:
The Allegory of the Female Form

From the Beast to the Blonde:
On Fairytales and Their Tellers

Managing Monsters: Six Myths of our Time
(The Reith Lectures 1994)

The Inner Eye: Art Beyond the Visible

No Go the Bogeyman:
Scaring, Lulling and Making Mock

Marina Warner

MURDERERS
I HAVE
KNOWN

and other stories

V

VINTAGE

Published by Vintage 2003

2 4 6 8 10 9 7 5 3 1

First published in Great Britain in 2002 by
Chatto & Windus

Vintage
Random House, 20 Vauxhall Bridge Road,
London SW1V 2SA

Random House Australia (Pty) Limited
20 Alfred Street, Milsons Point, Sydney
New South Wales 2061, Australia

Random House New Zealand Limited
18 Poland Road, Glenfield,
Auckland 10, New Zealand

Random House (Pty) Limited
Endulini, 5A Jubilee Road, Parktown 2193,
South Africa

The Random House Group Limited Reg. No. 954009
www.randomhouse.co.uk

A CIP catalogue record for this book
is available from the British Library

ISBN 0 09 942837 7

Printed and bound in Great Britain by
Bookmarque Ltd. Croydon, Surrey

For dear Jacqueline

'The more, by the bond of love, we enter into each other's mind, the more even old things become new for us again.'

Augustine of Hippo

Contents

Natural Limits   1

Canary   29

Daughters of the Game   55

The Armour of Santo Zenobio   63

The Belled Girl Sends a Tape to an Impresario   77

Lullaby for an Insomniac Princess   89

Stone Girl   103

Murderers I Have Known   119

No One Goes Hungry   139

Acknowledgments   163

Contents

Natural Limits

'E leven thousand virgins?'

'Yes, absolutely.' Bettina insisted.

'But the whole population of Cologne can't have been as big at that time.' Candace, laughing, was still tenacious. 'You did say the fourth century?'

'Oh, it was far smaller. Think of it like this: a palisade on a muddy riverbank, a smoking encampment, and perhaps a paved road. There wouldn't have been much more, then, in the ancient *Colonia Romanica*.'

'So the murder victims outnumbered the ordinary inhabitants?'

'You're being very literal-minded, *cara*.'

'And every one of them was killed?'

'Every single one. Brutally murdered,' Bettina continued, picking up speed. 'Chopped and split by the Hun. Like so much firewood. Memling painted it as a kind of prequel of the slasher movie.'

'Not everyone, in fact. There was one saved.' The young man, Rudi, Bettina's new PA, had been half-listening to her, but now he interrupted. 'She played dead.'

Bettina's eyebrows sharpened to delicate chevrons in mock

enquiry, and Candace gestured to him to carry on. But their turn came at the delicatessen and they began to choose from the heaped display of sausage, salami, and various other cured and treated meats spread out under the enhanced rosy lighting of the meat counter.

Bettina added, 'And I suppose she felt great remorse, of course, that she had not been martyred with the others?'

'This is the not-to-be-missed German cultural experience,' said Rudi, looking at the spread. Candace could now identify, in his voice, a recent stint on the West Coast. 'Not those old, dusty and kranky – no, you say sick – legends.'

The differing sheen of glass, of marble, of tiles, swam with liquid highlights as in a Dutch still life; in the food hall, some of the counters were barrows, and had striped awnings with gay dagging to match, others were sparkling crystal and steel frames as in expensive cosmetic departments, all were piled high and heavy, with bundles of root vegetables still attached to bouquets of top growth greenery, and authentically begrimed. Though indoors, the stands were disposed deliberately haphazardly, to create the semblance of a street market; frolicsome wild animals stood among the scene settings.

Candace pointed out a pale pepper-dusted *salame* and turned to Bettina for approval.

She nodded. 'You choose enough for us tonight. Make it a feast!' But she looked at the crimson, inky, veined and roseate pilings of cold cuts and sausage without enthusiasm.

'I leave you, Rudi, to guide our visitor around the varieties of *wurst*. I'm going to get the salad.'

'I mustn't eat too much,' said Candace, helplessly fixed on the spectacle of the massive rampart of charcuterie. 'It's all very well for you.' Bettina was wearing green silk shantung trousers, with black piping down the sides. Her mother had made them up for her from material which she had bought in Hong Kong. 'The excess of it. Who eats all this?'

Bettina's eyes, which were childlike in their roundness, tilted up to the corners when she was amused.

'Haven't you seen them – everywhere? The munchers, the grazers, the feeders . . . ?' She chomped with her jaw. But she stopped, worrying for her friend, who for a moment looked stricken. Candace was certainly heavier than the last time Bettina had seen her, and puffy in the face and neck. From drink? From clandestine eating? Or from quiet secret crying in the night? From doing all of these?

Bettina put her hand on Candace's arm. 'Come, the vegetables and the fruit are very good here.' She spoke English rapidly, with an Italian intonation; the magazine she published was printed in Turin, and her life and work there had blurred the German in her voice. 'They leave the earth on for effect, to make you believe in their extra naturalness. Then you're happy to pay more. But at the same time it works, the taste is better. *Vedrai*, tonight with Gervase, we'll have a wonderful picnic: carrots and olives and tomatoes and cheese and everything that's good for you. With champagne or schnapps.'

'You're bringing some?'

Rudi nodded. 'There's already some bottles in the trunk.'

'And besides,' Bettina carried on, 'you'll see Gervase will drink with us. He has an appetite under that cool, controlled exterior. He's a kind of a magician, and magicians have to experience everything in order to . . . deepen their knowledge. When we were younger, Gervase and I, before he went to live at Hollen, we tried to eat a toad together once. He said it was a species famous for possessing in its epidermis a certain substance, an antidote to all known poisons. He said we would never suffer from the effects of pollution again. He was always making big boasts like that.

'He managed a little piece. But I didn't have the nerve.'

Bettina and Gervase had been together one whole summer in the early seventies; there were still photographs of events they staged in various galleries here and there.

'But the whole point of this, *cara*,' she said, for she caught her friend's anxiety that she would be intruding on a lovers' reunion, 'is that you and I will have some time together, with no one else, mobiles off, no other calls, nothing, and I want to hear *everything*.'

Bettina Strahler never seemed to be running things; her manner was attentive, as if she were keen to follow others' directions and take instruction. But this was only a feint. If it weren't hard to compare people to dogs without sounding derogatory, thought Candace, Bettina was a beautiful pointer, with enhanced sensitivity in her ears, her nose, those delicate pricked arches of her brows, the tips of her fingers and the tips of her toes; yet she succeeded in being in charge. She was almost always subtle about it; Candace could think of no one who could create such quivering bright loops of energy around her as she moved.

When Bettina telephoned from Basel, Candace had risen to her suggestion, to make time in both their busy lives to be together, because, she told herself, she had to learn to be grown-up, and she needed a friend to convince her. It wasn't that Bettina was an obvious exemplar for growing old. But in the matter of growing up, she could learn so much from her, Candace decided, because she's gifted at staying alive, and keeping hold of life. And that means she has understood limits, that she has grasped them. She doesn't smoke, any more; Candace couldn't give up. Something eludes me, she thought, something precious and good about life itself. Like a child who won't eat because she hates the breasts growing on her thin ribbed chest, I can't make myself put away that childish thing, that flirting and courting of glamorous Mister Death, in his biker's leathers, with his smouldering eyes, his smouldering fag, his dirty fingernails. So it had become her New Year's resolution, to open herself to change, and to begin trying to survive. She was thinking of daily yoga, of weekly twenty-four lengths, of a polyunsaturated fat-free diet, a bathroom exercise bicycle, an office trampoline, nicorette blister packs, catalogues of outdoor protective clothing made of newly invented (patent-pending) fibres to resist wind and sleet and sun and salt, manuals of hiking trails, such as she saw in friends' living rooms, in magazines and papers, and through the blindless windows of street-level gyms. But still she couldn't overcome her repugnance for these attributes of proper grown-upness, and adopt even one of them.

Familiar faces that are now dead smile at me, she acknowledged, from the obituary pages more often than I expected; and acquaintances I thought far older that I am turn out to be several years younger, and there they are, gone to their long home. In the English papers they don't tell you what they died of; in America, where the topic of health has driven out other ways of seeing and everything has become either a hazard or a benefit, the obits close with the brief, melancholy envoi: of cancer of the bowel; of the ovaries; of the jaw; of AIDs-related complications. Tom (*your* Tom, as he used to say with heavy irony) keeled over with old age. He had almost everything. I got so sick of the list. But it was fundamentally old age. Used up. He had been used up for years.

Bettina put it to her. 'Come and join me, I am going to visit Gervase Mendoza in Cologne. We can travel together. You know, he has become very interested in death. And interesting about it, too, I think. Everyone should be, but we are all shy and awkward and our tongues go dry and our lips go thick when the subject arises. Artists deal with it better. Gervase is a new Grünewald: miracles and disease, together; angels and pustules; demons and rainbows. This metaphysic is still deep down in the German psyche; he has inherited it.'

Grünewald. A new Grünewald. Will he help me seize hold of death? Candace asked herself. Understand what had happened, to Tom, that it will happen to me? Unless.

Tom's white-grey crunchy bits unburned in the handful of dust. Like the bone meal sprinkled round the roots of roses in the spring. I must organise a ceremony, she resolved. Some friends, somewhere he enjoyed. A scattering, a mulch, then something growing in his memory. Something inscribed. *In Memoriam Tom Wendle. He loved this spot.* She used to feel choked reading such remembrances on benches in the park. You can only read them when nobody's sitting there, and this conjures the ghost very effectively. The thermos flask, the newspaper, the eyes looking up at the view. He loved this spot.

For an instant, she saw Tom very clearly: he was holding his temples between finger and thumb, as he did when his head hurt. She had never been sympathetic in the morning at his groans; she had migraine, which was the real thing.

It is so bloody annoying, thought Candace Parris, that I feel this emptiness now, when I never liked him, never, the whole of those five years together. But then I didn't expect to like a husband – that's not what they're for.

She had thought there would be more of them, too; perhaps not husbands, but lovers, 'partners', in the currently preferred, flattening term. Their scarcity, as it turned out, was to blame for her feeling Tom's death now. Twenty years ago, she spent so much time and effort avoiding men and sex and intimacy. Intimacy: the word used to strike her as indecent.

Now she realised, I am trying to understand this hollow inside me.

She rallied, all at once: there had been others, she mustn't come over all maudlin. It was just she was ashamed she had married, and married Tom of all of them; his dying now threw that relation into relief. Next of kin; he had named her, and it was, she supposed, true.

I am trying to understand this, thought Candace Parris. I am trying not to join him. I am trying to learn to want to join him and the others later, rather than sooner.

She could see Bettina was thinking of asking her to write about Gervase Mendoza for *Balcon*, her impeccably designed, trilingual art quarterly; or perhaps conduct a conversation. She was running a series of such exchanges, and had provoked much comment: in London, Candace had heard young PV crawlers in the latest geek polyester chic and lemon-yellow haircuts exclaiming at them. Most recently, she had published a trialogue between the Oldenburgs (Claes and Coosje) and Rachel Whiteread; before that, there had been tapes made with Louise Bourgeois and a Russian artist Bettina was supporting.

They walked out into the cold Cologne shopping mall, the winter biting small stars into the paving stones. They came to a square where a Romanesque church stood; wartime damage showed in walls of new slub concrete. They stopped and went in, and while Rudi went to fetch the sacristan, Bettina found a side chapel, and called Candace over.

It was frescoed with the legend of the massacre in High Gothic: the artist had a feel for fashion, for every tendril-haired maiden – and there were hundreds of them falling under the executioners' savagery – was swathed in beautiful, rich drapery, with rills of lace and silk undergarments swirling from brocade gowns, to reveal perfect shoes, square-toed in the latest court style, with wedge-shaped kitten heels.

The sacristan was ready for them now, Rudi came to tell them. A man in his fifties, dressed in a green felt hunting jacket with antler horn buttons was waiting by an armoured door which was buckled from age, bolted and padlocked; when he unfastened the heavy hasp, a narrow Gothic arch was revealed, with a dark, wooden, inner door.

He grunted as he found the light, but it was dim, and the smell of the chamber reached them before they could make out its contents, as of an old apple store that has been forgotten, so that all the sweet aroma has turned to wrinkled, webbed, pickling must. It was hard at first for Candace to see what she was looking at. The bones in the roof of the chamber weren't recognisable as parts of bodies at all, they were assembled in festoons and swags, so that they looked like some kind of baroque plasterwork. But then the vaults became legible, and she realised that the martyrs had all been jumbled and shuffled together like the heaps of the dead in genocidal wars. But here, in the vault, praises were written in the long bones and the forearms for the slanted shorter strokes of the letters: a femur for the upright on the T, a pair of tibia for the middle caret of the M: *Ave Ursula, virgo praedilectissima. Deo Gratias. Requiescat in pace.* There were armouries Candace had seen in the guardrooms of old castles like Windsor, which display weapons in similar patterns, but here the rosettes were made of shoulder blades, not bucklers, and the starbursts of clavicles, not scimitars.

Bettina whispered to her, her eyes mischievous, 'Very pious ladies did it all. Like pokerwork. Or that Victorian way of making straw pictures, you know. The V&A has some.' She gestured stitching with her fingers. 'In the tedious dark winter evenings . . . think of the deep pleasure; think of the *frisson*.'

For days, for weeks, for months, they must have worked, thought Candace, looking at the tiers of shanks and fibulae, as they pushed the bones around until they struck a design they fancied, then hooked them in place with silver wire, before hoisting the finished tray on to the ceiling.

They hadn't lacked for materials: it must have been the largest bone-yard anyone had ever seen when they first came across it long ago, during the building of the medieval city walls.

'So you think it was a bit like cuddling up with a horror movie at a teenage sleepover?' asked Candace. She thought of her friends' daughters, shrieking and squealing in a blissful kindle, at some monster foaming green wax from fanged jaws. 'The Cologne Ladies' quilting bee assembling eleven thousand dead women's bones?'

Bettina beckoned her over; she was tapping the walls where reliquary heads were stacked in niches, some of their pretty young faces painted pink and white, some mask-like, golden. Candace joined her, and peered in through the gilded baroque oculi that divided the niches. Inside each one, lavishly veiled in dust, there were skulls, shelf upon shelf.

Candace was silenced; then she whispered: 'Bettina, it's weird, weird and gruesome. Why?'

'Why did they do it? Or why did we come? Because Gervase's work is rooted in Catholic cult and ritual practices like this, and the form they take here. No carnival joking, no capering and thumbing your nose here; no singing and dancing, no Mexican Day of the Dead. The cult of death straight up. "Death is a master from Germany." You know, the kids in Berlin are writing that on the walls now.'

The killing fields of Cologne. Inside each oculus Candace could see the empty eyes of one of Ursula's band looking back at her, blindly, of course. Cézanne's great charnel portraits of his last years.

The sacristan was explaining something to them.

'Ursula was English.'

'She was?' the visiting Englishwoman exclaimed on cue.

'Yes, an English princess,' the sacristan continued. 'Something like your Princess Diana.

'And so were most of her handmaidens – so you feel home here, yah?' He smiled at her as he began to open one of the cabinets.

'Ursula was betrothed,' Bettina was now translating from

a leaflet, 'to someone by her father, a pagan. But she refused to marry a pagan.'

'Of course.'

'Instead, she sailed away in a boat for a year or two – with all her train, a flotilla,' said Bettina. 'Ten ships, a thousand virgins in each. They made landfalls, spectacular landfalls, on the way. In Brittany, in Flanders. Then they sailed here, up the Rhine, and came face to face here with the masters from Germany.'

The sacristan had unlatched the golden perforated screen that covered one part of the wall opposite the altar, and there, inside, were rows of skulls, like an anatomical specimen collection made during the rationalist vogue for palaeontology, for evolutionary research and brainpan measurements. But Candace saw that each of St Ursula's companions was visored, so that their deep and empty eyes swam above a purple mask as if over a yashmak; thick with dust, of course, the trimmings of gold lace gimp tarnished, after so many centuries since the ladies' industry had adorned them, they still displayed a baroque luxury. The sacristan in his hunting jacket took one off the shelf. He held out the skull in its silk bonnet and face mask to Candace.

'Esmeraria,' he said. 'Saint Esmeraria. She was Ursula's first cousin, noble-born, like herself.' He paused, holding the skull closer to Candace's face, as he nudged Bettina to translate. 'They played together as children, and she stepped in front of a spear to defend Ursula, crying, "Heavenly Father, I come to thee with gladness in my heart!" She was a Precursor, she was to Saint Ursula like John the Baptist to Jesus.'

He was warming to his topic, and walked up to the high altar of the chapel and picked up a glass vitrine, in which another visored skull was ensconced.

'Here is Saint Ursula's head.' He held out the relic in its glass dome to Candace.

Bettina said, 'You may hold it if you wish. It's a privilege. He can see you are a serious person who will understand.'

The sacristan urged her to accept his proffered treasure. The expression in his eyes was solemn, even slightly alarmed, as if he were defying his own better judgement.

'You know, she is the patron saint of migraines,' said Bettina. 'Because she was decapitated.

'Make a wish.'

'Bettina!' Candace protested, receiving the glass box with some reluctance. 'You're such a pagan. A prayer, that's what's called for. This isn't birthday cake.'

She took it, and looked at the cracks in the skull where the plates of the cranium were stitched together as if hemmed by a sewing machine. There was a round hole in the forehead: a wormhole? The same hand-embroidered visor covered her jaws; otherwise, she realised, all these skulls would have grinned and gaped like ghouls on a fairground ghost train.

Then she saw that, in contrast, the reliquary heads on the shelves beside them were showing their rosebud, gilded mouths.

And every one of them was smiling.

The skull in its glass box was making her feel very peculiar, queasy, and light and out of scale. Not least because she couldn't grasp why she was consenting at all. Here I am, she thought, in this gaudy charnel house, my Yorick no more St Ursula than a stage prop, a nameless ghost's skull in my hand, the ruin of some forgotten Roman from a jostling, exuding, phantom population murmuring at me through matter that's no more alive today than . . . what? Than a stone, a busted plastic bottle, a dented tin can, refuse, rubbish, there was nothing of Tom left behind in those scraps of ash and bone; nothing. He's only alive in my memory and in others', and even if memory is made of chemical spurts excited by grey matter, it's certainly got to be less material than this box, this skull on a pillow.

'It's made me feel rather sick,' she admitted, sucking at the cold air outside, once they had left the Golden Chamber and St Ursula's church.

They walked back to the car. Bettina was smiling.

'You're so perverse,' said Candace. 'You Catholics.'

'But you were fascinated, weren't you?'

Bettina was sitting in the back; she wanted Candace to see out, though there was little in view from the autobahn.

'I didn't exactly like it,' Candace said. 'And I don't understand. For me, the dead no longer exist. At least that's what I believe with my rational mind.' Out of the window, flat winter fields were dragged into a uniform puddled grey as they drove past.

'The rest is voodoo. I know.' Bettina leant forward to speak closer to her friend. 'Your Tom, then Allen, my friend Judith who committed suicide in the river last year, none of them exist any more. At least not materially. But it's hard to let go of the idea of getting through, isn't it? Touching those bits that were once . . .'

Candace protested, 'You sound as if you believe those bones really are what they're claimed to be. It's preposterous. How could you?'

'Gervase will make it clear. But you don't have to write anything, not unless you want to. It's just, you would do it – well, you would do it perfectly.'

There was a moment of quiet; the winter trees streaked by.

'By the way, Rudi,' said Bettina, 'tell us about the only one who survived.'

'It wasn't for long,' he replied, obedient. 'She was choked to death by her mother-in-law – with a silk scarf – just a few years later. So she was able to get together with the others, in heaven.

'But I guess she didn't get to be a full Virgin Martyr.'

The monastery where Gervase Mendoza lived was a disused brick works. Over the last three years, he had gradually filled the long central space of the factory floor with exhibits; the upper gallery, where the manager's office and other administrative areas had been, now contained his private apartment and the guest bedroom.

He came to the door as soon as he heard the car; he was wearing a cassock; the black cloth was rusty at the cuffs and hem, and stained with plaster and paint and glue and resin and other materials. His tense eyes were the kind that look as if they're lit up from behind, like in an advertisement for a painkiller. He kissed Bettina three times, saying her name, slowly, as if he heard such a name for the first time. His hand when he shook Candace's was chapped; his manner almost absurdly formal, as if he were receiving her on an official occasion. 'I am glad you have come to the Museum of Likeness and Presence. Please to sign the visitors' book. I am afraid that if I don't ask you to do it straightaway, I shall forget in the excitement of your company.'

The table contained a small rack of postcards, and a flat glass-topped tray in which a few objects were displayed. 'Museum Replicas', said the label. Candace noticed an enamel pin brooch of an eye, encircled by what looked like flames.

They presented Gervase with the wine and their offerings of supplies from the deli; Bettina arranged for Rudi to return the following morning to pick them up.

Then they were standing together in the entrance to the museum, in silence, looking ahead, into the exhibition area.

The moment of awkwardness passed; Gervase began handing out acoustiguides, and showed Candace how to tune in to the English translation.

'You will find it very easy to follow. This version takes only half an hour. I haven't yet completed the fuller account. I am composing it now. It will take much longer. For those who like to let their minds wander . . .'

The Museum of Likeness and Presence began with a peepshow: through a pinhole, you could see a tiny piece of fabric, set into what looked like a lump of rock crystal, which had the effect of magnifying it, as if it were an ancient incised gem too small to see with the naked eye. Music played on the acoustiguide, with choirboy sweetness; Gervase's voice, speaking softly, perhaps to lighten his accent, explained: 'The swaddling bands of Jesus were brought to Germany by the second of the Magi, King Melchior, whose remains still lie in the cathedral of Cologne, in a magnificent reliquary that comprises 1,436 cabochon stones of Hellenistic date, mostly originating in Asia Minor and other parts of the ancient Greek empire. Melchior, who was over a thousand years old (longevity was in the family, as it still is in some parts of the eastern Steppes), presented the swaddling bands to the grandfather of Carolus Magnus, who preserved them in a precious coffer that is only opened for one day every two years. However, the Museum of Likeness and Presence was able to locate a piece of the miracle-working cloths that Melchior had kept back for his own use. It was handed down in the female line of the family of the Gräfin Adelheit von Kreuzeningen who was gracious enough to donate it in her grandmother's memory.'

Candace unlatched the device in her ear, and found Bettina, who was standing listening in front of another vitrine, in which was coiled a rope, with some miniature white roses growing beside it from a seeming fissure in the earth that covered the floor of the showcase.

Bettina forestalled her, pointing: 'The rope which the famous fakir something-or-other-Nandy used to climb up to heaven in the year seventeen hundred and something,' she said. 'He always left behind him an elusive scent of roses. So we have the flowers.'

Candace giggled. Then she noticed that the roses weren't real. They were so delicately rendered, almost tremulous, that they must have been cast from the real thing by lost wax, and then painted, or enamelled.

Gervase Mendoza had worked before as a restorer; Bettina had done the same course in fine art conservation techniques in Rome in the early seventies, and they had been friends since then, as his international reputation as appropriation artist and culture guru grew. Recently he'd established his Museum of Likeness and Presence, his Wunderkammer, his cabinet of curiosities, and visitors were beginning to make the journey into the countryside near Cologne in greater numbers. It remained a mystery how he survived; the entry charge was nominal. But then he truly lived like a monk, as he claimed to do.

'The thing about Gervase now,' Bettina confided, pausing her machine too and moving Candace towards another case, 'is that he will never depart from the role he's assumed. The likeness he presents is the truth. He wants you to believe that there's nothing else lying veiled behind, and in many

ways there isn't. However much you try to make him tell
you – ask him to talk normally, to say what he's doing, what
he's up to exactly – he won't. I don't even know any more
if he thinks he's playing, or not. He'll tell you he's in charge
of a small, little-known museum of sacred icons and relics,
he'll insist that he was appointed by his order, and there's
no more to it than that.'

They were now looking at the flaming enamel eye, the
original of the replica in the Museum Shop.

Bettina turned on the tape again and fixed the earpiece;
Candace did likewise.

'The eye is the lucky jewel,' said the steady, accented voice.
'Found in the brow of the toad when the princess in the fairy
story lost her golden ball down the well and he retrieved it
for her. Some say it is the pineal eye which experiences the
wonders which the eyes of the body cannot see.'

Bettina touched her on the arm. 'You see, that's the clue.
Gervase always had a thing about toads.'

The cabinet contained some more predictable items: a
unicorn horn, a stuffed mermaid like many found in animal
specimen collections of the seventeenth and eighteenth
centuries; a curling, crumpled horn that had grown from
the forehead of a certain Magdalena Duckers.

Candace remembered those freak shows of her journey
through the States many years before, 'Ripley's Believe
It or Not!' in which Houdini's stunts were reproduced
alongside photographs of bearded ladies, the Most Gigan-
tic Amethyst ever mined, and the slippers of the Chinese

Cinderella (two and a half centimetres of flowered satin).

In an aquarium some cone snails were crawling over tiny pebbles: Gervase's commentary explained their venom produced such a deep sleep that the victim would appear to be dead, and that certain celebrated resurrections may have occurred after an unsuspected encounter with such a snail. The creature's method was to stun any obstacle with its slime.

'This is true, I think, by the way,' said Bettina. 'And these are real snails.'

'I don't think so,' her friend replied, keeping her eyes fixed on the moving forms. 'The pattern of their movements repeats. Watch. But how's it done? With magnets? With electronics?'

'The method is part of the mystery, I guess. Gervase is rocking your deepest sense of stability, undoing your bearings in reality. He wants you to know wonder again, and in that way to see God. That's the point, like it or leave it.'

Candace no longer wanted to cry out against it; or at least that wasn't the only response. She wanted to laugh. She was laughing. It was a funny feeling, loose and wild, and the image of a kite passed across her mind, when the child flying it lets go, and it bobs away, jerking in the wind and gaining height till lost to sight.

Gervase accepted the picnic Bettina had brought, and indeed, it seemed as if he would have overlooked the question of eating altogether otherwise; he took pieces of sausage and tomato and he drank Bettina's champagne, rather obediently and frugally. But the stubborn consistency of his play-acting – if it was play-acting – made him flat company; it reminded Candace of visiting heavily sedated friends in hospital after a crisis; she was soon floundering about for a topic that would crack his apparent automatism. Bettina had infinite patience with artists and their idiosyncrasies, it was part of her job, she said, and however obdurate their pretence or their mask, she remained interested. But she was alert to Candace's need for her comfort, and so she soon announced that they were retiring, and drew Candace off to their cell early.

Neither woman had yet lost their parents; so they were still someone's children, and for this reason perhaps, they were able to sit together like children on the thin mattresses side by side, tipped towards each other across the gap between the beds by the sagging chainlink hammock of the bed frames, and Candace smoked, and dunked the butts in the washbasin when she'd finished. Bettina talked about the friends she had lost; and the loved ones. She made it possible for Candace to think, to speak, to face their absence with her. We have lost so many, thought Candace, but somehow this hasn't taught me to accept what's coming and change my ways. Bettina's eyes searched out that space in the middle distance that is also somehow that recess of memory deep in the back of the head where the lost loved one can be made visible, still moving, still talking; her vision became wings for Candace, that she could fasten to her ankles, to her cap, so that she too could follow. She may be as incapable of being sensible as I am, Candace was thinking, but she doesn't evade the issue or pretend the worst hasn't happened: one form of blindness doesn't, in her case, throw a cast over the whole of her sight, as it does with me.

'I didn't go to Tom's funeral,' she finally confessed. 'I was ready, I was dressed, and then I couldn't make myself. The undertakers telephoned afterwards. I was so ashamed. They were calling to make an appointment to deliver the urn.'

She was able to admit it to Bettina, her terrible failure. Her denial, as a therapist would call it. Bettina knew; friends had told her, Candace herself had rung her, late one night and left a wandering message on her machine.

Candace was saying: 'But the last time Tom and I slept together was 1986. And that was a mistake. I never considered myself attached. Not really, not properly. But I turned out to be, you know: "A little more than kin and less than kind."'

Bettina put her head on one side and one of her delicate eyebrows contracted. 'Why are you reproaching yourself? Tom could have been having a joke: it sounds like one to me. To send you his jar . . .'

'Urn.'

'Urn, of course. *Urna*. A kind of comic revenge of the discarded lover. The sort of prank you get in low Italian fables. Boccaccio-style misogyny.'

'For what?'

'For sleeping with him in the first place; or, for not sleeping with him since 1986. I don't know. I never sleep with anyone now. It's too complicated.'

'I don't either. But not because I've made up my mind not to. I'm cursed with heterosexuality.'

Bettina threw back her head with laughter. 'You should be happy about that – the fires not dim yet!'

The sound of feet shuffled down the gallery towards their door, followed by a tap and Gervase's voice calling: '*Liebe Bettina!*' Bettina's eyes danced over her hand as she smothered a laugh.

'Gervase! At this time of night!'

Candace tried to straighten herself; to run a brush through her hair, brighten her lips and cheeks.

'Come, I have something to show you!'

'We're coming,' Bettina sang out. 'Just a minute.'

He took them along the gallery, now lit only by the glow above the doors of their bedroom and from the frosted glass windows of the former manager's office cubicle, his closed apartment's antechamber.

'Your eyes will soon become accustomed to the darkness, and you will see better.'

Gervase reached for Bettina's hand; she gave Candace her other and the three of them seemed to tiptoe through the darkness of the museum's central nave towards the end. There, in a new glass box, was the shape of a head apparently made of gold, for its edges flared, though the rest of it was black. As they got closer, they still couldn't pick out any features, and when they were standing, almost with their noses to the glass, there was nothing in the case except an oval glow suspended over a small cushion made of plum velvet.

'Bettina, and you, too, Bettina's dear friend, you are the first to see the greatest treasure the Museum of Likeness and Presence has been fortunate to acquire. Just keep your eyes steady, as if looking through the case, past it, not trying to pick out anything in it, and you will begin to see something.'

In the dark, Gervase's low, stilted speech made Candace half-giggly, half-jittery; she began to feel cross-eyed as she tried to adjust her focus in the way he described. Bettina still had her hand in Candace's; Candace was glad of her touch; her string was now held firm, she felt earthed.

Then she saw it: it materialised in front of her eyes just a fraction before the same gasp of pleasure escaped from Bettina's lips.

'You cannot photograph it,' said Gervase. 'It's an image which has no reflection. Because it's not made of light, but only of deeper degrees of shadow. So the only place you can see it is here, and in this darkness.'

It was a kind of a face; it was a pair of eyes and a pair of lips; above all, a smile; a smile dreaming to itself in space.

'*Acheiropoieton*: made with no hands,' said Gervase. 'A relic so rare I do not think it can be found anywhere else but here. It is the true likeness of a soul in paradise, caught permanently as an impression in the air, in the same way as you see matter dance in the rays of the sun.'

'Did you notice something familiar about her?' Bettina whispered to Candace when they were back at last in their funny gimcrack beds with their dipping supports.

'The seraphic smile?'

'Yes.'

'It's his most beautiful piece so far. So ethereal. Visible and invisible. There and not there. Like and not like. Present and not present.'

'If there were eleven thousand of them,' Candace said thickly, through waves of tiredness, 'there's no reason not to have turned up another, I suppose.'

'*Eh già, vero.*'

'Goo'night, Bettina.'

'Sleep well, darling Candace.'

'You too.'

'You're glad you came?'

'Ye . . .'

They were both drifting now, coasting through another kind of dark.

Candace Parris was stiff when she got back home, from a bad night trying not to toss and creak and disturb the childlike slightness of Bettina asleep, and from having sat on the runway in the crowded plane while some passenger whose bag was on board remembered to catch the flight . . .

and then she'd taken the crowded tube from the airport and, in the interests of health and beauty, carried her bag the ten-minute walk to her door from the station. But she was still happy, she was still drifting, still laughing; she went to the kitchen and found some washed salad left over in the fridge which hadn't browned too badly, a couple of small tomatoes and a jar of mayonnaise lite. Then she brought down the urn which she'd pushed to the back of her wardrobe and took some of Tom's dust and ashes and sprinkled them like pepper on the mayonnaise; she loaded her fork and bit carefully, reverently, expecting a tart, metal pungency, something like semen but dry. The flavour was elusive, so she took another two dressed and seasoned leaves, but found that they tasted no different.

Canary

W hen he first came to London from a small town in Delaware, one of those American states most people in England can't place on the map, the word was that he was sexy. He had thick hair which corkscrewed; even then, when he must have been in his late twenties, the Heathcliff-like grimness and metallic blackness of this pelt was lightened by little twists of silver, and his jacket was dusted with loose scales of dandruff. Close up, he sometimes smelt of zinc-rich shampoos with which he tried in vain to control it, and he would dash an impatient hand at his shoulders; women frequently flicked at the scatter of flakes from his scalp absent-mindedly. You could tell who he was sleeping with when they showed this unconscious intimacy, touching the traces his body left.

Manley had been to Vietnam. Though almost everyone who met him then was against the war and had been on the Grosvenor Square march and even bound their brows in headbands of torn muslin in emulation of Viet Cong mourning rituals (so it was believed), and although these protests were not exactly insincere, Manley's career as a grunt was terrifically interesting to almost everybody who heard of it; it, too, made him sexy, to men as well as women. His friend Pinch – they went everywhere together – used to throw quiet looks at him with those funny pale parrot eyes of his, which are baggy above and below and show the whites all round the iris; he was studying him, like an actor picking someone to imitate for a part. Pinch was – is – much more active than Manley when it comes to numbers, but he felt then that he was short on style, I think.

I first saw Manley in a half-lit backroom at an artists' party – I forget where, or whose party it was. But I first remember half-lying, half-sitting beside him on an Indian mirrorwork textile spread on a low couch, both of us drowsy from the fumes of patchouli cut with grass which you still sniff around stick-thin beggars working the tube. Manley seemed very grown-up: he is in fact a little younger than Pinch, but older than most of his other friends in that gang, all of whom had coincided at the same college in different ways. He never did talk about the war. But he did talk about brothels and prostitution in far distant places and he had a provocative theory about casual sex and its pleasures and its costs. People always demurred, of course, but wanted to hear more. And if you were a woman, like me, who thought that sex for free (I'm old enough to call it 'free love') was a sign of liberty and that liberty was civilisation, you were outraged. But you didn't forget Manley. Or the shiver of jealous inquisitiveness his experiences produced. His defence of the bordello was an insult to Us, but it seemed to hold secrets that tantalised: that bought women are better at it, better at giving head, at displaying, at crying out, at squeezing and scratching here and there – these were the pictures that came up in my mind's eye as if I was in the mean white room with the Madonna on one wall and the girlie calendar on the other that Manley described having visited in Da Nang.

That night however he was talking about Gutenberg, and about Wittgenstein and language setting the limits of the world; he was chuckling that experiences which escaped the net of words could not have happened.

Sean was sitting close, on his other side, wearing a feather necklace, and he'd had his hair dyed blue in homage to Andy Warhol's silver. Pinch, Manley and Sean: they were the new set, the new style, the new art, going into forbidden zones without flinching, and the rest of us were groupies, I suppose. Some of us were artists, too, like Cosmas, who made sculptures with aeroplane parts, and Branko Pec, who'd come to London a refugee, and was Jessica's most constant concert-going companion, as Manley often worked late and didn't want to interrupt a painting to hear music. But it was the three of them, because they were younger, because they were tougher, too, who set the pace; they outdid one another in defining the temper of the times. Really, they were rivals, but they'd decided to be buddies (though Manley would never use a word that implied as much sentiment, even if it was the favoured US Army term for the kind of homosocial bonding that he, Sean and Pinch had forged together).

Sean Starkey was the most talked about of all: he'd even sold out his degree show – a sequence of oil paintings about the hero Gilgamesh's drunken rampages and his passion for the wild man Enkidu, all set in grey rainswept streets of an L. S. Lowry smokestack cityscape and terraced miners' cottages. Manley tapped his friend on the thigh, and said, 'Do you think queerness doesn't exist if there aren't any words for it?'

'Of course it does. It happens.' Sean spoke slowly, in a Potteries accent that managed to be simultaneously blunt and drawling. 'In silence, in the dark, you don't need words, or pictures. There's a kind of knowledge that's got roots somewhere else. Skin remembers. My skin does.' The younger artist closed his eyes under his crown of blue. He was short-sighted and when he looked at Manley again, his pupils were very open: 'The rest's a load of bollocks.'

'Slang dictionaries,' Manley went on, 'show mankind's inexhaustible inventiveness when it comes to sex. But even so, I bet that most people learn from what they hear – and read – and pass on experience in that way. Art runs ahead of life.' He raised his head to address the room. 'Don't you want to have all the lives you read about? To be Jack Kerouac one day, Stephen Dedalus the next? Polymorphous! To escape the plan that's written there, in your DNA?'

He was working on a series of prints at the time: portraits of Famous Men for the Long Gallery in the *musée imaginaire* he was assembling, he said. He was going to make a miniature version in a box, and sell it as a multiple. But even while he was laying out his high plans, I couldn't help thinking about him in the jungle of Nam and in the peepshows and whorehouses of Da Nang, and this is what happened, I think, to almost everyone who sat down near him, couch or no couch, mirrorwork bedspread or no.

'Can I think beyond what I can say?' Manley was holding his hands out in front of him as if speaking with them. 'Does it really hurt me when a man says to me "I'd like to see you dead"? Why do women shake and tremble when a man whispers obscenities at them down the telephone? Or curses them from a car for failing to indicate a turn? "Fuck you, asshole!" Why does that make my pulse pick up? When a critic writes, "This man isn't an artist, everything he touches is hideous" – does something actually happen? Am I wounded? Do I bleed? Words –' He went on stabbing the air like the punctuating top line from the trumpet when the melody's unfolding below. You felt – *I* felt – that sex was the inevitable outcome.

But in my case it turned out it wasn't inevitable at all, because I was friends with Jessica, whom he lived with, then married, and she and I eventually became close, though not as close as she wanted, I think. This was partly because I wanted to keep the door to Manley ajar. I should admit that when I saw Jessica (which was far more frequently than I saw Manley) and as I began to sit for her I kept on hoping that I would see him and that we would talk and I would be able to tilt my friendship towards him rather than her. Or that he would like her paintings of me because they were of me, or that I looked especially fascinating, as if I were one of those dowered princesses whose images were sent to possible bridegrooms in the courts of Europe, and were unveiled – the curtain drawn aside – and the prince gazed upon the face and was captured. (I am trying to be honest, and honesty frequently means owning up to the banality of one's desires.)

I sat for Jessica for days on end, over two or three years, it must have been, but intermittently, as I didn't have time to go daily. Like all the artists in that group, she always had several canvases going at once, so that when one model was available she could resume that painting, and so on. (Pinch had made so much money he had different studios on the go, too, with different models, and, it was said, different lives with them in each.) I would take the Number 31 bus to her studio – which was in a large ground-floor flat with duck blinds floor to ceiling on the front bay. In their ideal pristine state these blinds had a pale silver crinkled glow on them like Japanese rice paper or like that common biennial, honesty, which can set miniature full moons softly radiating in the flowerbeds of damp spidery London gardens in October. She had two sets of them so she could send one to be cleaned, because the smuts from the traffic load outside slipped through the window frames, past the outer sash and through to the gap between the double glazing, where they accumulated and from where they seeped into the interior of her painting space, tingeing the cool selvedges of the blinds with grey dust.

The studio was seductive; it separated you from all other concerns, and sitting for Jessica emptied your world of everything but her and you, together, one opposite the other. She talked a little when she was painting, often of the paints themselves, their character, their quality. She sometimes squeezed them straight on to the canvas and then dipped and spread them from there; she loved the slide and give of the brush in the pigment, she said, as she dragged an outline into a blur.

In the first portrait, which was called *Anya, West London*, I looked oddly cheerful, I thought. Nudes are serious, on the whole, unless they're Beryl Cook butterball belles. But I was lying on a couch, on a quilt, gazing straight out – and I was trying for a kind of Olympia look: Jessica was an open admirer of Manet. My body was slightly swaggering in its nudity, and my face didn't show a trace of that inward rapture of self-absorption that the female nude traditionally communicates, in Old Masters and centrefolds alike. There was a touch of Third Reich naturism about it, I thought privately – a kind of pink healthiness and physical assertiveness which I didn't feel had much to do with me. But it had impact, in its disavowal of any anxiety about middle-aged flesh in the buff. It was festive; celebratory was beginning to be a buzzword at the time and Jessica's paintings were indeed just that.

But that was the trouble with them as well. I told Branko as much: 'Jessica is so insistently upbeat about everything. It gives her work a kind of fake sunshininess. In that painting of me, I feel like an outsize apple in a supermarket, displayed under a pink bulb and sprayed every now and then to keep it glossy.'

Branko was indignant, and it was probably stupid of me to criticise Jessica at all to him. 'There's absolutely nothing faked about Jessica's sunniness,' he almost shouted at me. 'She *is* happy. When she sees happiness in others, she doesn't feel her innards contract with envy the way we do. God, how can we all be so twisted that even sunshine has to be ironical? Or some kind of a cheat? For Jessica, a sunshiny day is a sunshiny day and she rejoices in it. But you've just become cheaply cynical and brutalised – like me, like the rest of us.'

His forehead was slippery with sweat as he burst out with this; yet Branko of all the group was the artist who painted the most forbidding images of all: cross-hatched thickets of lead white and lamp black for familiar parts of London as sites of ongoing atrocities (he had been born in the Balkans, he had racial memory, he said). But Jessica was soothing, even to someone as hackled as Branko.

As I say, Jessica paid attention to the present moment and its immediate offerings of rewards: that delight in the ooze and squidge of the paint from the tube, that mother-of-pearl capsule of her studio. She had a large, clear look, wide eyes under a high, unlined brow and rain-coloured hair which swept back and down in a soft springy fall; the kind of formal harmony of face and figure that could be showered on, windswept and dishevelled and only emerge enhanced, like beach pebbles. But she was kind with her beauty, and never pressed her advantage. I know this, because she liked Ian quite a lot and wanted us to sit for her together, and when we did so – only three times, as art isn't his scene, and he felt awkward stripping down in front of a woman painter – I fancied I could hear her calling to him with her brush. She painted his cock so lovingly, I was surprised when I saw the results that it hadn't risen up then and there to the squeeze of the paint and the dab and push of her brush-strokes.

Ian is twenty years younger than me, and I think it embarrassed him to become a spectacle, a partner in an ill-matched couple, like in those cautionary images of a warty old lustbag and his beauteous paramour (with her hand in his purse). Jessica wanted to celebrate us, she said: 'You're an example to us all, Anya,' she'd cry. 'None of this giving up on life and love at the age of fifty . . .' Personally, I welcomed the chance to lie with Ian for hours because his body had properties for me as crystals do for New Era adepts, or multivitamins for health addicts, or taking the baths for my grandfather's generation back in Austria. He has a kind of fresh briny smell as if he had been swimming in some sea before the motor car was invented, before the industrial revolution, when the word pollution merely meant ritual defilement, menstruating girls in temples, not soapy poisons frothing on the tideline and the river banks. His body hair is soft, and in the studio light, I could see its springy spirals fringing his edges against the milkiness of the interior lighting. This all sounds OTT, so I'll add that he was one of those men who are much more appealing at very close quarters than dressed: he's an ordinary thirty-year-old coffee-coloured Londoner from across a room, with twists of scrappy hair on his head and a tendency to puffiness about the eyes and waist from the statutory quantities of beer that media boys and girls have to put down after hours. (Ian's a photographic technician in a studio I use for colour processing and other jobs.) I enjoyed lying still, curled up against him for one of Jessica's paintings of couples – she posed him so that he was spreadeagled, legs making an upturned V centre-front, so that there was no avoiding his genitals as the focus of the composition. I was an incidental form to his glory, and though, as I say, I half hoped that all these images of my body were going to be appreciated by Manley when he finally got to inspect them, I could see that I had to take second place to Ian's dark young prodigality of flesh.

By the way, it proves how wrong that old idea is – that old excuse – that a man's cock has a mind of its own. From our position prone on the bed, we couldn't see Jessica; she was concealed behind the canvas and only became visible when she hooked her head round to scan our joined skins more closely. An erection isn't involuntary in the same way as sweat or bruising, whatever St Augustine thought and everyone after him believed about unruly concupiscence and the primal curse. The signal has to pass somehow through the brain.

But was Jessica really an *ingénue*? She seemed so. When she wasn't wearing overalls to paint, she favoured dirndls with embroidery and rickrack. Branko had given her an original antique one from his part of the world, and the heavy cloth, when it swung against her limbs, revealed a girlish, slim neutrality of flesh, edenic in its simplicity. She spoke in a soft slow voice on the telephone, and her manner was subtly cajoling, so that agreeing to her invitation or request was like settling back on pillows plumped and patted for your head in a children's game of Hospital and having bandages tied with soft fingers around make-believe injuries. The same feeling of a game came over me when Ian and I were posing as lovers for her – that we were playing Mummies and Daddies, as my brother and I used to do, lying together on the bed pretending to do what grown-ups do at night but not knowing what the mystery was or how to enact it for real. This was disturbing – here was a woman in her forties who could make you think thoughts that you quelled, blushing, in deference to her childlike innocence of manner. Yet how was that possible? When she liked to paint her models naked, and spreadeagled in close-up?

As I see it now, it was because I am devious and cynical – though not more so, I think, than anyone else – that I didn't trust the simplicity that shone from Jessica's mouth and eyes and murmured in her gentle voice. I suspected she was up to something.

Her parents had been sixties flower children – she had been brought up on a retreat inland from Big Sur in wilderness forest. They were both therapists, who used hots springs, hallucinogenics, Gestalt psychology, Masters & Johnson's sex findings as well as a vegetable garden and glasshouses filled with crisp white mooli and hairy okra and cherry tomatoes. They had a cage for raspberries soft and dimpled as babies' toes, and a small orchard where the fruit could be picked from the branch and where wigwams were pitched for special meditation sessions in solitude. (This is how Jessica described it – I never got to go there.) They treated patients on long weekends or short-term courses, and they were highly successful all through the seventies and early eighties: rock singers with custody cases, actors with a cocaine habit, record producers whose most lucrative group was insisting on breaking up, couples who wanted to raise the temperature in the marriage bed, came to the farm and helped to cook and serve the communal daily meal at the table where Jessica's genial white-haired, white-bearded father presided.

She had had a very happy childhood, she always said. Everything had always been explained in a level tone of voice; nobody ever lost their temper; when they did feel angry, her father told them to use the anger positively, to turn it into energy for good – towards work, towards others, towards sex, towards providing for self. The housework and gardening the patients did was part of the anger management training. It was highly effective, too. For the kind of guests who came to Swallow Hill were used to having servants, and the chores were a kind of game, not an interminable sentence of drudgery; they were playing Houses, if you like.

But Jessica's craving for art wasn't fulfilled by this life, and when she wanted to leave, the parents gave her a bit of money to live in London and study. There was still a lot of northern California about her: she liked drugs – smoking dope, mainly. Again, this seemed rather a youthful taste, compared to my Irish malt, Ian's bitter or Manley's vodka.

I always imagined they had an open marriage, Manley and Jessica. Brothels still figured in his conversation as the supreme testing ground of the male libido. When he started in on the subject, Jessica simply bent over her cooking more intently, as if her hair could stop her ears as well as hide her eyes when he set off on a dithyrambic hymn to the Rue St-Denis. 'The whores are real whores, no half-measures, no camouflage. In nothing but their bra and knickers and lace-up boots, right out on the street, letting it all hang out right there on the pavement: not the sweet sentimental rag-and-bone shop of the heart, but the charnel house of lites, of the gut, cunt and cock, naked, no pretences. They're fat and old and still juicy, those Paris whores – oh, the ballsiness of it. That's a real trial of a man – getting it up, faced with all that. It broke my heart when they shut down that street. Nobody comes clean about anything any more, about the inalienable darkness deep down in all of us. That's lust, that's the pity of it, the truth of it – no quarter. That's the severe discipline that you find in the greatest metaphysical writers: in Dante, in his Inferno, with the sinners grabbing and gnawing each other in the ice.'

Jessica revered him. I wondered sometimes if she was like one of those mystics who insist on wrapping themselves in a bug-infested blanket, but remain untainted and unharmed, their inner purity proof against all contamination. I was drawn to Manley's hardness because I sensed I was one of his kind, using my camera as a shield to go into experiences for that rush of pain that makes your body palpable to yourself, that undoes the everyday numbness. But Jessica didn't seem to see that aspect of his character. When she talked about him – and she did, often – he was a tender, vulnerable, older man, rather frail, a genius who depended on her strength and her calm to bring out his full potential. The possibility of her infidelity (with all those models) kept up a steady and subtle threat, and the brothel talk was his way of retaliating. That much emotional management Jessica had certainly learned from her father and mother on the farm.

'Do you feel possessive? Of your lovers?' she once asked me. We were walking across the Park together, on our way a summer or two ago to a show of Paula Rego's at the Serpentine Gallery. It was one of those London evenings when motes fly gilded on the breeze under the broad-boughed trees and the voices of children and strollers and others float and mingle.

'Well, sometimes, I do, yes.'

'Is Ian faithful?'

'I don't ask.'

'Have you been faithful to him? Because you want to be?'

'Oh, Jessica!'

I wanted to say I didn't get that many opportunities, as in my world almost all the young men are gay. But I restrained my impatience. She was also childlike in this prurience she admitted so casually – she wanted to poke in and look underneath matters adults usually keep quiet about. She and Manley did have that in common, I suppose, though their styles were different.

'*We*'re not, you know.'

'I know.'

'I like sharing. It makes me feel close to all the people I love.' Under the guise of handing me Manley as a present, was she asking permission to sleep with Ian? But I knew that it wasn't up to me to accept my side of that bargain, if Manley preferred to pay, and pay for them fat and juicy and naked on the street. That was when I withdrew from the closeness that was developing between us.

But I am forgetting something. As if in one of her paintings, I'm looking at Jessica in close-up and I'm failing to give a sense of the position she and Manley occupied in the larger view.

In one of the portraits of me, I'm holding a photograph – Jessica had thought of including a camera but she didn't like the thought of it near my bare skin, she said. The image would suggest my career without violating the conventions: it was a group photograph I'd taken of the boys' gang – Manley and Sean and Branko and Cosmas and of course Pinch – which had been published in *Vogue* in the sixties and since then had been republished any number of times in histories of those days, and, just recently, reprinted in an issue of the *New Yorker*. The magazine asked me to shoot the gang again, but it proved impossible to muster them – Sean was in Santa Cruz and Cosmas was too frail now to come up from the beautiful old monastery in Gloucestershire he's bought.

The artists in the gang all painted in the traditional way, in oil on canvas, from the model, or from observation elsewhere, but because they were bad boys, poking about in newly distempered parts of *la vie moderne*, they weren't like stuffy RAs painting the English garden – though many of them have become RAs. The group took as their motto, 'To be with art is all we want', and they came to be known, rather grandly, as the School of London (some of us dubbed it Fog & Snog). There was debate about which of them was the greatest living painter now that Francis Bacon was dead, but nobody disputed Manley was the brains of the group. Most of them commanded higher prices than Manley, however; Sean, who was of course still the youngest, had always been the most popular with the public, and has remained so, though he's fallen under the influence of Jeff Koons and taken to painting portraits of his cats in pink bows in the style of Fragonard.

Although Jessica met all the criteria of the 'School', she was nevertheless held in an undefined exclusion zone. The many articles written about the group usually mentioned her ('Jessica Bernice, also an artist, married to Manley Finestein'), but she couldn't cross the invisible barrier into the boys' club. Like them she painted from life, she explored forbidden areas imperturbably. They loved her – and not just Manley and Branko either. She was successful, too, in showing her work, in getting commissions, in selling, in having her pictures reproduced and distributed. One of her paintings of lovers in a London park was taken by the Tourist Board as a poster, then became a T-shirt, a souvenir mug, the cover design on stationery, and so on. But she wasn't one of the group.

She didn't complain. When I think of her now I see her in a patch of light, like the bright yellow streak she used as highlights in the scatter of sun and shade on the ground in a painting in the park, and her head is on one side as she listens to the men, and she's smiling, gently, at what they are saying; but I can see that they are wrapped in murk, and their voices are breaking up, like a lost station on the radio. She doesn't notice this separation between herself and them; she continues to sit quietly, delighting in them, approving them. It's a cliché, I know, but Manley could do no wrong in her eyes.

In the last days of that summer, Jessica had the show I found too sunny. It included two paintings of me – the double one with Ian, and the single full-length holding the photograph.

Manley stood by his portrait to be photographed for the Sunday papers – not by me. Afterwards, at the dinner, the talk was mostly about his forthcoming retrospective, which was to fill the new Gallery of Modern Art, in the immediate wake of a big Philip Guston show. This was going one better than Pinch, whose most recent exhibition had been held in the old Tate, and who had not (yet) been offered a full survey in the magnificent space of the new GMA. Manley was planning to fill it with his *musée imaginaire* in which he was going to pay homage to all the influences on him – 'the *Upanishads*, the *Odyssey*, *Finnegans Wake* – and, of course the Cabbala, the Torah, and the Tanakh, as we Jews call your Bible'. He laughed, genially. And looked around the table at the faces smiling with him: his grand manner amused his friends, but none of us shared his cultural aspirations. Pinch had left school at thirteen, and had the handwriting of a window cleaner, and those of us who had been educated valued education far less than Manley. He had done a correspondence course in philosophy after he was shipped out of Vietnam; he'd also been going to weekly classes in Hebrew for years – and made Jessica go with him. He was making slow progress, but Hebrew ciphers appeared with more and more frequency in his paintings.

'The show will be thematic,' he was saying. 'In three parts – "Silence, Cunning and Exile". I'm going to embed my pictures in context in each of the sections, with quotations from the Masters. It's time we stirred people up a bit! To the possibilities! To a new canon out there – this country is still pig-ignorant.'

I think now we failed him – no, we failed him and Jessica – because we let him run on, and didn't issue any kind of challenge to him or suggest restraint. We didn't warn him not to antagonise all those pig-ignorant guardians of culture. It's strange, but Jessica's total tolerance of him silenced any move on her friends' part on his behalf. Her acquiescence drew us in like a contagion: she didn't raise a voice to say, How can you talk like that about prostitutes, when I'm right here? She didn't get angry with his failure to include her as a fully-fledged member of their group. She'd learned too well to channel the energies of frustration. And their double attraction over us all paralysed us in reaction: I was maimed, I must admit, by my continuing fascination with Manley, and my low spark of jealousy that she had designs on Ian made me fail to champion her. She was an innocent, good and sweet and beautiful and talented, and that's a lethal cocktail: underneath the most loving friendship, there remains a deep pull of mortal envy.

But perhaps my weakness didn't arise from this rank ground. I remember once being on a beach in Italy, and a couple with a small child were about twenty feet away. They began tormenting the child, who was playing in the sand next to them. They were lying on a towel and together they pulled the boy – he was naked, about three years old – towards them, and shouting at him, the mother began slapping him on his bottom and then the father whacked him over the head, screaming at him. The child began to wail and try to pull himself away, but the father lifted his arm and said, 'If you don't stop that now, I'll shut your mouth.' My heart was bumping under my ribs, I wanted to rush up and grab the child and wrap myself around him, like a human shield, so that they couldn't touch him without dealing with me first. But then I had an inspiration, and I grabbed my camera out of the polythene bag in which it was wrapped, screwed on the long lens and stood up to take their photograph.

The clicks shut them up. But I didn't know if I'd simply driven their violence behind doors; if next time, they'd slap the child around in private so nobody could shame them by looking.

But I never said to Manley, 'Do stop being so fucking overweening, so fucking self-aggrandising.' And I never said to Jessica, 'Manley is a monster, and, besides, my darling, you're the truer artist.'

I'm not blaming myself, or anyone else, as there are limits on friends' intrusion into privacy, and a marriage is a sacred space, whatever degradations it has suffered, in which visitors take off their shoes and bare their heads and join in the liturgy as performed by the celebrants, rather than impose their own ideas.

Nevertheless, Manley plunged headlong into an exhibition of himself while Jessica stood by, gently acclaiming him at every stage. And when the blows came raining in on him, it was she who took the brunt of them; she was the personal assistant in the ministry who opens the letter bomb, she was the canary who is carried in a cage through the terror-stricken streets of a city after an unknown cult has poured liquid gas on the pavement to poison the air.

Manley Finestein: The musée imaginaire was a huge show; its opening marked the high point of the artistic year. He selected the work himself – he was very autocratic, and people, as I say, were scared to give him advice, even in professional matters. That was the first miscalculation. The second was that he insisted on giving sources in the original language, with translations: the wall captions included Greek and Latin tags, German gobbets from Kant and Heidegger, Danish for Kierkegaard and even Chinese and Japanese for various lines from Chuang Tzu and Zen. He intended a deliberate provocation: Manley included an enormous painting of the Death of Keats, in which Keats was a self-portrait. The wall caption read: 'Artists who have wisdom and are ahead of their times are never recognised by the philistines who set the standards of the day. My work and I have always enraged art critics. This painting is an allegory of art's inextinguishable vitality and a memorial to the poet John Keats, who was killed by a review.'

The painting showed Keats in a space superimposed on a photograph of the steps of Trinità dei Monti in Rome. The dying poet was wearing Manley's trademark red-and-white check work-shirt and braces and was surrounded by figures who – as the key on the wall explained – represented contemporary artists in the guise of their precursors. So Shelley's recognisable delicate features were given to a body holding a palette and brush with a beribboned cat on his knees (Sean). And so forth. Various newspapers and magazines were lying tattered and stained underfoot, crawling with lizards and flies and a rat or two. At the private view, Manley was helpful with explanations: 'Lizards don't do anything but lie in the sun, like our contemporary art commentators, fat on their salaries and so lazy that it's usually necessary to poke them to see if they're actually alive.'

The Gallery of Modern Art should have stopped him, could have stopped him, perhaps. But he was obstinate and hard to gainsay. The critics could have laughed – at the sheer effrontery of it. He was like a drunk picking a fight with them, and they could have ignored him, and looked at the work. But they didn't. An eminence in the art world delivered his verdict: 'Finestein has the best brains of a golden generation of British art. But as an artist, he can't draw a figure that doesn't look as if it's falling apart.' Even those papers which never usually cover art leapt in: 'Go back to the US Army, Manley! Or didn't they teach you to look down the end of a pencil?' *Buzz*, the television late-night arts show, summed up: 'A has-been, a no-talent, a wannabe Wittgenstein, the grand old man of transatlantic art, Manley Finestein might as well go down to the Job Centre. That's the verdict in the London art world today.' In *The Times*, an investment adviser warned: 'Contemporary art can be an invigorating risk, but in the case of Manley Finestein, the bungee rope is liable to snap.'

Manley withdrew into his studio and shut the door. Jessica had to call him on the intercom from the front door to talk to him and he didn't always answer. She was sick with worry, and she asked us, she wanted to know, Why had they attacked him so ruthlessly? Was Manley right that the English hated foreigners, especially Americans, and more especially Jews? Sean told her that it was like they used to say about the blacks: 'In the North they say, "We don't mind them going high as long as they don't get close", and in the South they say, "We don't mind them getting close as long as they don't go high." Manley riled them, he went too high and he's got too close. That's why I left England, do you see that now?'

It was while Manley was in retreat that Jessica died. She was dealing with his mail about ten days after the opening, and she found the weekly papers' notices, including a review by a critic whom they had counted on. It was no better than the rest, and it hurt more, because he was a friend and had changed his mind in public without saying so in private.

When Manley did appear that night, for some food, Jessica told him she had a bad headache. He wanted to know what the weeklies had said, if the picture was improving at all. She told him it wasn't. He picked up the journal and read his friend's condemnation of his work, and went back into the studio.

The funeral service took place some time before she was buried, because the need for an autopsy meant delays, and that is contrary to Judaic rite. In the synagogue, her male friends were each given a little paper head covering. I had never heard a cantor sing live before. His laments were beautiful, throaty, and I cried when I saw Manley on the other side of the room looking so haggard and wild-eyed and thin, and when the rabbi said Jessica was like the moon, reflecting the sun's light back on earth in kindly, silver rays from heaven. Pinch came in late and stood awkwardly to one side, his pouched eyes drily glittering. Sean read a poem

Jessica had once illustrated. Jessica's father flew from San Francisco, though he is very old; he said afterwards that there was maybe a strain of something in the family: his great-aunt had died suddenly of an embolism, too. But he shook his head, and added, 'These strokes are of the spirit, and the body is just the spirit's vessel, which cracks with it. It was the malice she couldn't bear. Jessica believed in human beings, in love, in kindness, in goodness and she believed art was all these things. We brought her up like that. But London's no Swallow Hill, and she found out she was pretty much alone here with those beliefs. I guess it killed her.'

The interviews began again soon after, and Manley told the journalists, 'They were gunning for me, but they got her. I have work to do, and when I've done what I was put on this earth to do, I shall kill myself.'

I rang him up once or twice; but it was hard to connect to him, and I stopped trying. When I bumped into one of his studio assistants recently, she told me he's coping.

Daughters of the Game

The stand-in could now take the place of the actress under the rain machine; Faye Lavery was going back to her dressing room to rest until the close-ups. She beckoned her hairdresser and make-up artist with a flick of her wet hand; they ran to her, took up position on each side of her and made as if supporting her to her quarters.

The director called her back, and she turned, making her weariness a plain reproach to him.

'I'm going to have bruises tomorrow like Mike Tyson after the big fight.'

'That's why we're going for the scene – the whole of the scene – today.'

The stand-in walked over to the puddles in the fake tarmac under the dripping lee of a SoHo fire escape, and looked over her shoulder for someone to take her dressing gown. Underneath, she was wearing the same, light, swinging, summer dress as the star, with a leaf pattern in white against a burgundy ground, and fastening of small mica buttons down the front. They were sewn on to press-studs, so that when Jed Lester, the male lead, pulled at her from behind, the buttons flew off easily.

The male lead and the stand-in were to perform the next segment of the scene in the rain, which Faye Lavery had refused to do. He had to throw his right arm round her stand-in, under her chin and twist her till her body was bent backwards into a stretched arc. When he practised, the director saw her ribs lift and part slightly, like the fragile lips of a pink scallop, and he whispered an instruction to the lighting cameraman.

'That's how I'm meant to flip her around,' Jed Lester whispered to her, 'And then – well, you saw – I grab her like this, and . . .'

The director came over and pushed her head back so that it was hooked over backwards against Jed Lester's shoulder, and then moved his right arm higher, so that he looked as if he was holding her in an arm-lock. Then he moved the actor's left arm down to her groin.

'Flex your hand. Yes, like that. Good, perfect in fact. That's the basic position. Now, let's shoot.'

Jed Lester's face would stay in view; the scene demanded his grimace of pleasure. She – his Cressida in the director's remake of Shakespeare's *Troilus* – was his whore, and the director wanted the brutality unbuttoned.

'You, Jed, think of something you really like. I want an expression of pure bliss on your face, animal ecstasy. You're appetite, the kind that cries hungry from the pit of the stomach and wants what it wants with no other thought. You're lust, greed, tyranny let loose upon the world, the enemy of innocence, the end of hope. This is the deed of darkness.' He laughed. 'Just give this scene all you've got.

'Now, you . . . ? He hesitated.

'Fernanda,' said the stand-in, relaxing out of the pose, and throwing him a tentatively friendly smile, since she was working for him for the first time, and liked his films, admired the elaborate excesses of his aesthetic, his grotesque and unlovely visions of the damned. 'We both begin with F –'

A stand-in had no face, she had a thousand faces. Fernanda had gone to drama school, and registered with an agency as a model. She acknowledged she would never be used as a cover girl, she didn't have those kind of looks. But she had a figure, and she liked it being seen. Soon, casting directors came to know her work: her legs and her arms were in demand. Standing in for Faye Lavery had followed: Faye had a baby and a habit and the one had darkened her nipples and the other had puffed the skin on her body, on her thighs and upper arms especially.

The eventual film, which was called *The Pandar's Scrip*, reached a huge audience after its release, in spite of the incomprehensible title and the rancid, unremitting cynicism of its squalor and savagery, because the Americans refused to grant it a video certificate – not even at their highest exclusion rating. So a small-budget, bizarre art-house movie based on a lesser-known Shakespearean drama became a twenty-five-million-dollar grosser and a cult movie. Projectionists took out their razor blades and snipped the reels for prized souvenirs. A frame from the rape in the rain became a favourite trophy. Faye Lavery's naked body in the gaping dress, arched and forced from behind by a modern Diomedes, turned into an icon of the high street. You couldn't see her face, just the actor's hands, one jammed across her parted ribcage, twisting her right breast, the other shoved down against her crotch, bringing her onto him, with her head thrown back and her thin neck aquiver and stretched, and a glint of tooth, above the strange taut apex of her upside-down chin.

It had been a closed set when Faye Lavery was playing the events leading up to the rape, but the technicians were back and busy checking the rigs and the lights during Fernanda's scene. Still, some of them later remembered that she had stood in at the crucial moment of the notorious shot, and when they bumped into her, at a screening or a trade party, they'd nudge her knowingly. Some would say she'd missed out there, and yet others would urge her to take the case to the union and get some money for her famous ribs. It was now being bootlegged by art students and designers of fanzines and CD covers; it was rapidly becoming, on this side of the fin-de-siècle, what Monroe in *The Seven-Year Itch* in those white ray pleats lifting over the subway grating had been in the fifties. But Fernanda laughed, as if at the very thought of it. 'Look at me,' she'd say. 'Think that's me?'

She had two small boys now, growing up, and she wanted to keep from them the knowledge of this kind of work in their mother's past. But also, though she hardly put this into words herself, she wanted to remain fluid, a woman with many faces; she did not like to be recognised.

The image came up in discussions about the prevalent complaisance of the media with open incitements to rape; Camille Paglia retracted, on several programmes, that she had ever said that women liked rough sex. Jed Lester made a public service broadcast, earnestly advocating the use of condoms. The director expressed no surprise that his attack on the scabrous decade had become merely more fodder for mass fantasies. He would not offer any apologies: the obscenity was not of his making. He was merely a pair of eyes, a pair of ears. Faye Lavery, for her part, frequently expressed heated indignation in interviews when 'that shot' came up, which it always did.

Then the photograph appeared in an international advertising campaign for a famous brand of designer jeans with a witty and lubricious *double entendre* in the slogan. Faye Lavery sued; she pleaded mental distress at the image of herself raped in that way circulating round her wherever she went. The defence of the designer jeans and their advertisers had no difficulty finding plenty of witnesses who, for reasons they did not quite understand, found it rather satisfying to testify in court that the famous image of Faye Lavery had not been posed by her at all.

The stand-in was traced; Fernanda was called to give evidence. Afterwards, when she went to pick up her boys from school, they and their friends looked at her curiously. Faye Lavery was awarded damages, all the same, as the jury decided that her grievance was genuine since everyone thought that she was the rape victim. The advertisement was withdrawn, but the company did not care; it was felt that the image had now lost its aura.

The Armour of Santo Zenobio

They had a quarrel; then there came a shower in the square and they took shelter under the arcade opposite the small museum on the harbour piazza adjoining the *duomo*. Studiedly, she read the inscription on a tablet above them on the inner wall: she wanted to show him she had a strong, separate existence and could find interest in life aside from him. But she couldn't help exclaiming at what she read there, and so the silence between them came undone; they began to move to each other's breath again, woodwind, a chamber piece, quiet and urgent. They had returned to their room in the hotel on the sea front, and as he remembered now the way Julie had leaned over him and thrown her hair over her head and let its soft bright rain sweep his body as she whispered his name, he heard her again say it, 'Fabio', and his answering, involuntary moan floated up through him from the past.

Dott. Fabio Gremoli had not been back to the town since then; now, as he lay in the hotel, he found himself awake before daybreak, remembering. He pushed open the shutters; Isabella had telephoned to tell him she was detained by a meeting; she would join him, for sure, the following day. She ran a business in leather goods; made money; took telephone calls on her mobile at night; while his architect's firm in Milan was idling.

The dawn drew light pleats slantwise across the sky, which was still deep and dark; he recalled Isabella's underclothes, which were severe but expensively tailored to pull against her hollows. Angry that the journey they had planned together had begun without her, vexed that she was always so occupied and keen to let him – and others – know it, he had not wanted to arrive at the house alone, and so had stopped in this small port on the coastal road, where he had not made a reservation, which he knew only a little.

He began looking for the tablet; it was fifteen, no, maybe twenty years ago, that Julie had come upon it and her pleasure at its story had calmed their anger; she now had children, whose mutinous faces pulled a smile in occasional Christmas cards she still sent from New York. There was the inscription; he quizzed it. It described a miracle, and Julie had laughed at its unlikelihood.

He did not read monuments, because he had worked since his youth in cities, where every corner recorded the moment when a leader on an arduous march had made a halt to drink from a well, proclaimed the founding speech a father of the state had given from this very spot on the pavement, or admonished the living to recall bloody sufferings. Summoned in his language's oracular past historic, the commemorated dead – the lost heroes, statesmen, artists and poets and musicians – were usually so local and so minor that the statues became indeed their only claim against obscurity.

But Julie was a stranger, an American in Italy, a student, and she liked puzzling out the rhetoric.

He'd pull her away: 'It comes from that creaking old humanist tradition – *liceo classico* and all that. *Democrazia Cristiana* pieties – so bombastic – disgusting – how can you bear it?'

But this inscription had made even him smile; had softened him:

A gunboat had appeared off the coast over two hundred years ago and opened fire. The square was packed, it was a Sunday, and the 'solemn noonday Mass' had just finished, when 'a blazing cannonball' had hurtled through the air as if 'from the very pit of hell itself'. The crowd had no time to scatter, hardly even time to realise the danger, as the 'fatal missile' came roaring among them, but never reached its target, never landed on them, and instead rose up again in an arc, high into the air and hit the wall at the *piano nobile* of the arcaded palazzo on one side of the square. It did it some damage, cracked the stucco, shattered a window, before burying itself toothlessly in the brickwork.

No one had been hurt. It was providential; the mercy of God had spared them.

All this was told in the condensed sharpness of that literary tense. It was a pity, Fabio Gremoli found himself reflecting, that everyone used auxiliaries now, just as they made buildings now full of slack spaces and decorative features. Such verbs, so abbreviated, so staccato, seemed to cut deep into memory till it bled more brightly. But almost instantly, he dismissed the thought, ashamed at his lapse into nostalgia. Memorials made the history seem real – as if with fake gore, he thought: the public, smiling wounds of agreed histories.

The tablet did not say if the gunboat repeated its fire; perhaps its other missiles had fallen short, into the sea, spouting there like sea serpents. The incised stone words closed by thanking heaven and Santo Zenobio, the town's patron saint, for preventing a massacre; by the grace of almighty God, the Blessed Virgin Mary and all the saints.

For the miracle was not that the cannonball had simply fizzled out; it was that it had hit the town's patron saint on the head. It had landed on him and then bounced off; or, strictly speaking, it had been repulsed by the armour the statue was wearing: Santo Zenobio, piercing a small, gnarled and scaly dragon with his sword, was encased in heavy, loricated plates of chased steel. The cannonball had landed on his head, and though the helmet of his visor was up, it had ricocheted from that impregnable surface and begun to fizzle out.

The helmet had been a bit dented, Fabio remembered. He turned to look back at the church; the morning light so near the shore was delicately flossy now, like dandelion spores, and it rose up from the smoothness of the sea; the meeting of air and light and water was indecipherable in the shimmer. The monument in front of the church looked unfamiliar. He walked over: his first impression was correct. Here was no longer their valiant knight in armour from a decade or so ago; but a substitute, a portly statesman with his hand raised, holding a diploma, in a bronze swallow tail coat, cravat and waistcoat, and the stamp of the foundry beneath his booted foot.

The church was open; the usual four women and a man at the early morning Mass. It was nearing its close; Fabio called in at the sacristy, where he found, as he'd expected, some postcards of the miraculous statue and holy pictures with a prayer on the back invoking the intercession of Santo Zenobio. He wondered what furious local outburst of anti-clericalism could have led to this disappearance, of a patron saint who had saved the townspeople from a massacre? How had Santo Zenobio been removed from his pedestal?

Fabio Gremoli had no time for the Vatican or its faith, but it offended his sense of history to see the miracle effaced; besides, the story was connected with that journey, with a time when he had not realised that such love-making would not be his for ever, had not understood there would not be so many others like Julie, or feelings of his own to match what he felt then. He was a son of the post-war consumer boom; he had been formed to expect products to repeat, exactly.

The priest who gave him a half-dozen of the holy pictures was seamed in hands and face; his teeth showed when he replied, smiling at his visitor's interest, like an old dog's; his cassock was smeared.

'I'm all alone here, now. But when I came there were six priests, besides me, the novice. Now everything is up to me – there's not even a woman left to dust the altar steps. Otherwise I would show you Santo Zenobio. He's in the crypt.' The priest pointed down, through the marble floor.

Fabio became more curious, and picked out a rosary from the pile and took out his wallet. 'Maybe I can go and see him by myself? Just tell me where – and maybe turn on the lights?'

The priest took the note, counted out change. 'Where did you say you were from? You can see Santo Zenobio's armour in Pisa now: in the Museo Diocesano.'

At first Fabio thought, wearily, Do I want to hear more, do I want to involve myself in some parochial tale of government and injury? But then he found he was asking, 'His armour? Yet he is . . . below? How so?'

'When I first came here,' the priest took up the question with unexpected heat, 'I understood straightaway that this armour was very particular – No, don't mistake me. Not because it is or ever was miracle-working. We are moderns, you understand, men of my generation in the church – moderns.

'No, I recognised it when I very first set eyes on it: a complete suit of armour from the skilful hands of Lotario Bartelli from around 1495. I knew it anyway, but I researched, I turned over documents in the archive; I found the name, in a ledger, with the sum, thirteen *scudi*, for the suit of armour. The original commission! Years passed before I could do

anything about my find. The name means nothing to you?
Tssk, he was the greatest armourer in Lombardy, worked for
the Visconti in Milan, a German by birth, Lothar Bartel, you
realise. And the sword! His signature on the blade in a device
of wyverns, in honour of Santo Zenobio's victory over the
foul fiend . . . ! Anyhow, I prayed to the Madonna as to what
I should do . . . and at last she revealed to me – in a dream
– that my only recourse was to make my discovery public.
Write to the newspapers, she commanded me. What am I?
Who was I? Nobody: a parish priest from a small place. But
I knew I had here a treasure of national interest. One must
do something when one knows what is right. So I wrote to
Il Corriere (even if it is owned and run by the devil and
his associates), and told them it was a crying shame that
this incomparable masterwork of the Renaissance should be
exposed to the elements, battered and rusted and falling to
pieces in the open. It was only a matter of time before it
disintegrated altogether, if nothing was done . . .'

Two women had appeared in the doorway, and were waiting patiently for the *parocco* to stop talking; each of them was
carrying a statuette. They approached, murmuring; Fabio
Gremoli estimated that the younger was about eighteen.
She had plump bendy legs under a skimpy dress, while the
other, too old to be her mother, and too young to be her
granny, was wearing a black lace mantilla that had turned
ginger with use. They thrust the coloured plaster figures
towards the priest.

'Bless them, please, Father, for our house.'

He raised one of his sere, cracked hands over the statues and began to mutter.

'No, Father, not just like that. Please do it the proper way, with the full ceremony.' The girl propped up her statuette of Our Lady of Fatima, so that the Madonna was standing upright and pushed her towards the priest, then made passes with her own hands, miming ritual gestures. 'We want you to make them holy, to give us protection.' The older woman echoed her; her St Anthony of Padua with baby Jesus in his arms was also stood up and held in place just behind the Virgin.

The old priest frowned. 'I haven't any holy water left; I haven't had time to make any recently, and if it's run out this isn't the moment to make some more.'

His brusqueness was startling to Fabio; but the women wheedled.

Under his breath, in the direction of his visitor, the priest threw out, 'These things don't interest me.'

But he crossed the room and peered into a stoop on the opposite wall.

'Come over here,' he beckoned the two women, pulling a stole round his neck and dipping his hand in the dribble at the bottom. 'You're fortunate it hasn't completely dried up. Otherwise, I would have sent you away.' He threw a glance at the visitor who was so interested in Santo Zenobio, and who was still attending to the array of goods for sale as he waited.

When the reluctant minister had finished the blessing,

he dismissed the women with a flick of his fingers; they continued to ignore his impatience and thanked him as if he had regaled them with kindnesses.

'I was successful,' he said to Fabio, picking up the thread of his story, his whole attention fixed on this outsider who was interested, and Fabio felt a certain surprised gratitude to him for staving off the habitual assault of boredom. His own company, he had never learned to enjoy it, as friends advised him adults should learn to do; he liked a companion, often if only to define his own apartness and lack of need. 'And my friend,' the priest continued, 'he wasn't my friend then, but he became so – came from London to verify my identification: the world's greatest expert in Renaissance weaponry and armour, Professor Oliver Stallworthy—' He paused, waiting for recognition. 'You don't know of him?

His visitor had to shake his head. 'I'm sorry, no. Not my field, you understand.'

'We took the suit down together, piece by piece, and cleaned and polished the rust and the grime off every one. It took us night and day for nearly a whole month. Then we looked at the figure underneath and realised we could not leave it on the plinth . . . he was made of straw and linen.'

In the crypt, the body of Santo Zenobio lay on its side. The stuffing was coming loose from the sacking which formed the torso, and the legs were bundles of sticks and straw tied with dried grass, also drifting into shreds. He had been flung, wooden head face down, as if drowned, so his expression could not be seen.

'Do you ever travel to London? You do? Will you tell him – tell the *gentilissimo* Professor Stallworthy – that you have seen me, here, in the parish of Santo Zenobio, and that I shall never forget his visit, when we ascertained that the armour was the genuine work of Lotario Bartelli, every particle and piece from his hands, no inferior stuff 'from the Workshop of', as is common. The Professor is an historian from Oxford – but he was already retired when he came and authenticated my suit of armour – he said it was one of the finest he had ever seen, with hardly a link missing from the chain-mail or a screw in the armour. And he singled out as his crowning masterpiece, the sword, the sword of Santo Zenobio.

'But the Professor has not written to me for some years now. You must go to the Museo Diocesano in Pisa – there you can see how together we saved a major opus from destruction. I would like to go to England, I would like to talk to the Professor again. If you go – everyone travels everywhere today – give him my homage. I have never forgotten what we did together those days.'

The neglected, ancient priest followed him into the square with his talk, but did not emerge from the darkness of his church. For his part, Fabio Gremoli was glad to be back in the light, now full and yellow as it fell across the stones, drawing a short hard shadow from the substituted statue on the stones of the piazza; he welcomed its dazzle, but put on his dark glasses to look out, eyes leaking from the brightness, beyond the square over the sea; out past the chiasma of breakwater and harbour wall, to where the separation of air and water vanished at the blurred boundary. In his own past historic, were there revenants as vividly present to his eye, rising from his core, as that armourer who had thrown down a saint and diverted a priest? He pushed the thought from him; statues, memorial plaques – how sure they were of their ground; he disliked them especially for that brand of lying.

Not that he was in love with ruins; he was a 'Modern' too, and had in his time raised many an austere interior of steel white plaster and glass, making no concession to the retrieval of memory, to the claims of nostalgia. Yet he discovered that he minded that he could not find it in himself to touch sharper, deeper, indelible longings or losses: for he ached only vaguely for Isabella's cool limbs, and Julie was a wisp, fugitive, as if his memories were painted in watercolours.

The Belled Girl Sends a Tape
to an Impresario

To Lynton Orlowski, Esq.
The New Stage Company
London WC1

From Prof. Sir Roger Scott-Mandell
Royal Cary Hospital
Clepton Shallett
Gloucestershire

29 December 19—

Dear Mr Orlowski,

Ms Phoebe Jones is a patient who has been in my care for several years now. She saw you interviewed on BBC2's *Late Show* the other night about your recent production (as did I) and your message about the therapeutic power of performance and participation in the theatre struck a chord with her, for reasons which will become clear when you listen to the enclosed tape, as I very much hope you will do. I also hope that you will not find this approach an unwarranted intrusion, for may I say that I too was very impressed – and indeed, moved – by the way you

---

reached out to those who are so often kept out of the light, as if society (and we are none of us free from blame) were ashamed of admitting them as members, as one of us. (I need hardly tell you that the disorder from which this patient suffers – formerly known as dysmorphobia, but since redefined, more properly, as body dysmorphic disorder – does no harm to anyone except the patient herself.) Through your work you are making splendid moves to turn this tide of prejudice and change attitudes and I and my colleagues here and, indeed, in psychiatric hospitals all over the world are deeply sensible of your pioneering enterprise.

I wish you much continued success with *The Gentle Giant* and hope that you will be able to listen to Phoebe's account of her life. I think you will find it fascinating. As they say, *Nihil humanum* . . . you are doing wonderful work.

Yours sincerely,

Roger Scott-Mandell, KBE, MD

Dear Mr Orlowski   I hope you will listen to me on this tape I am sending to you   Dr Roger says he knows how to get it to you   he nodded when I said you would understand me because I understood everything you said   every single thing you said speaks straight to me   you and me are brother and sister   flesh and blood   or perhaps born at the same hour on the same day you in Kansas City   I think you said you were born in Kansas City   and me in Bristol. Star twins that's what we are. From what you said I know we have identical souls and that you could take me away from here like you took those boys you were talking about away from

the place they were sectioned   no   perhaps not sectioned.
Kept. I am kept here   too   and I could do things for you
like they did. I can speak   you are hearing my voice on this
tape   I hope it sounds nice I'm talking to you now   I have
a nice voice everyone tells me so   it has a tinkling sound
like spring water   like fairyland! But I'm running ahead of
myself   I must take things one at a time and try and not
things get jumbled up. More haste   less speed that's what
the nurses like to say. You said that one of the boys you
took away from the place where he was kept couldn't even
talk at all when you started. You made noises and suddenly
you screwed your face up your mouth and eyes all twisted to
show us how difficult it was for him to make words. Your face
looked so different when you were showing us his handicap.
Handicapped   that's the word for it   that's something else
I'm going to come to   in a moment. At one moment you
were calm and beautiful   your face smiling and smooth
like the angel with the candle in the chapel here where I
go sometimes to ask that someone like you comes and lets
me out of here. You drew with your finger in the air a cube
and you said it was made of glass and sparkled and that your
theatre was like that an imaginary place where everything
was clear and pure and safe and beautiful and then you
showed us a photograph of him   of the Gentle Giant in
your play. Casey   his name is   you said and you could
hear what he was saying through all those funny noises
that heehawing and spluttering   Amy who often sits beside
me in the day room does that too sometimes   when we're

meant to be having quiet time. But you could understand what was lovely and wise and deep underneath and in the heart of him inside that horrible mumbling and stuttering Casey was doing. And he was only twelve years old then eight years ago   you said when you first took him in. The audience loved it when you told how you'd asked the judge if you could adopt him and the judge said   No   he'd have to go to a home but you said it would cost the state so much more money to do that than to let him go home with you instead. It was easy to see you loved him. Well   I know you could understand me even more because I   you see   I can talk to you. And I can perform   you wouldn't even need to teach me to dance and play. I can do lots of numbers   I've had lessons. I can twirl and ring the whole of the Beatles's first album   She Loves You Yeah Yeah   Love Love Me Do Money That's What I Want   and I Wanna Hold Your Hand that's funny really. But my audience likes it. I'm used to big applause. I'd spin round and round and take my curtain call dizzy from the public's love. Casey you said was a star you made him the star of your show   there was a photograph of him   sultry eyes   big slick quiff of hair and snake-tight jeans on a throne with a long drape flowing down the stage from beneath his feet and the light falling on him like a halo. Well   I would do anything for you if you did all that for me. Because I loved you when I first saw you last night on the telly. And you haven't tried the same with a girl   not yet   have you? Well I am the one. Lynton! Mr Orlowski! I'll be much better than Casey who couldn't speak   not

properly at least. You can hear how well I talk   I swear
this is all just coming out   without anyone helping me
no doctors around   I'm on my own   just you and me and
the machine. I can also scat a bit when I sing too   I am
fearless when I am in front of my public. I will be perfect I
will perform I won't flag I'll dance and sing   here   listen!
Just a verse so you know what I can do!

She loves you yeah yeah yeah
Hear the bells?

This is for why   I'll tell you the story   it's simple really
but lots of people don't believe me when I tell it. That's why
I'm sending you this   because you will. Like you could see
through Casey's noises   you'll see me. And then you'll know
I'm made for you to take away with you. That it wouldn't be
like two people together   but just one person. Two bodies
yes   but joined in one soul.

I was living in Bristol   I think I mentioned that   in a
small house with a garden front and back   no weeds in
the tiled path to the front porch   my mother always hung
the washing low so that neighbours wouldn't get a peek at
our underwear   so she said. The school bus stopped just
down the road   and I had time to run out when I heard
the driver turn the corner changing gear. I'd plaits then
which Mum used to do for me with ribbons tied over elastic
bands   otherwise they'd fall off because my hair is really
silky. And when she did her nails she'd let me do mine
too   dab it on for me. I liked the smell when I waved
my fingertips about to dry them   like Mum did. Frosted

Rose was her best colour   I think   but Cinnamon Gold
was good   too. Sometimes I'd do different nails different
colours   you know   to try them out.

   On Thursdays   I wouldn't come back with the others
on the bus   but go to my ballet lessons. Miss Morris   she
used to tap our feet with a little wand to make us stick them
out at the widest angle and hollow our backs and pull in our
bottoms. Tuck that tail in! she'd bellow. I had very expressive
hands   she would say to the class   and point at them with
her wand   and sometimes lift my arm a little with it to adjust
the pose in the mirror. Sometimes she put one of my
hands   they were small and quite pudgy then   in her palm
and then she'd stroke it smooth   like it was covered in
velvet with the pile running one way   and then she'd
bend the fingers down and lift my arm and check in
the mirror and tell the whole class to look at my *port
de bras* and stop being such heffalumps and take a cue
from Phoebe Jones. You can see I was her favourite.

   Miss Morris had small feet and the elastic of her ballet
slippers made her instep into two plump mounds like the
halves of a peach   she wore thick pinky-brown tights too.
When she was young she'd been a character dancer   she
once played a mad nun who tore her clothes off at the Royal
Opera House. Her brother   you probably know him   is
the actor who plays Kevin in *Streetwise* at 5.15 on Thursdays
with a repeat on Monday I always miss because it's my time
in the hot baths here. Miss Morris smelled of fags and talcum
powder all mixed up. One day she came home to see Mum

and Dad and told them I had a future and should go to a proper dance academy. So that's how I came to go to London when I was still titchy.

My hands were my 'passport to success' more than my legs Miss Morris said. She advised me to build on my strengths. They're your capital   darling   she'd say. This was when things got weird. You see whatever people were saying about them I couldn't believe. Friends in class would hold theirs up next to mine and the nice ones would groan and cry It's not fair! and the not-so-nice ones would look squintily and tighten their lips and I could feel their hate slam down on my hands like a hammer. I won't repeat what they said you'd think I was boasting. My boyfriend then was Lucas Tring   one of the Tring family   you know them too that   meant something to me   music hall   circus   dance showbiz   for generations   and he wouldn't let me do any-thing kept looking up insurance brochures to see what was the best deal he could buy to 'cover any loss'.   He stopped me even washing my tights in the basin saying he'd do all that for me so that my hands wouldn't spoil. He and I were renting together off the Earls Court Road and that's when things began to go really weird. No   I suppose they had been for a while   except that I hadn't noticed. He was an artist   he kept on saying   and I was his muse. He was planning a show   he wanted to be someone like you   Mr Orlowski   I hope you're still there   he was designing the lights and the choreography it was a puppet version of *The Little Mermaid*   with my hands in whiteface dancing the

parts in a black box like a Punch and Judy booth. But I kept
not doing the movements right. I kept falling over myself.
I was all fingers and thumbs! And he was shouting at me.
Then he'd grab my hands and massage them with oils and
breathe on them and he wouldn't let me use them even to
you know   when we were in bed. He'd wrap them in silken
bags with ribbons at the wrists.

I knew my hands were deteriorating every day   minute
by minute that if Miss Morris saw them now she'd notice
they were getting wrinkled like an autumn leaf and the pores
showing like someone has pricked out a paper pattern in the
skin. The joints thickening and the tips flattening and the
colour changing under the make-up   so that liver spots
were just round the corner. I was beginning to find it hard
to show them at all. I began pretending I had cramps so that
I could get out of appearing   not have to perform any more.
I stopped functioning really. Then one morning I woke up
and I couldn't move. I could not lift a finger literally.

I was lying in bed   though it felt as if I was lying kind
of above the bed   suspended like the girl who gets sawn
in half at the circus and a doctor came to see me and he
gave me the idea for the cure. He said I should have a
transplant   it would be simple. Plenty of people would be
glad of a pair of hands like mine   they'd be very useful to
someone   even if they didn't do me any good any longer.
He had a big black hat with a wide brim and silver buckles
on old-fashioned shoes and black stockings and he spoke in
a soft voice   he was an American   like you! I helped him

draw a circle round me with white chalk in my space above the bed and then I closed my eyes. There was no blood. He put my hands in a shoe box   wrapped in the neckerchief he had been wearing   and they did look beautiful   the knuckles dimpled just so   the backs smooth as ivory and each finger gracefully angled in relation to its neighbour. I was proud to be giving them away to someone who would know how to use them.

My bells play very prettily. You know bells are very unusual instruments lively with lots of character. My left bell rings in C and the other in F sharp which makes a lovely solid chord   rings of sounds that go out and out for miles around me   humming high and low and just a little bit dissonant   which gives an edge to my tinkling   I can tell you! I can play almost any song-and-dance routine you care to name   and I'd be pleased to   especially for you. So I'm still a wonder of the world   a singing ringing girl. Lucas always said I was his muse. But I'd rather be yours   Mr   Orlowski. Oh do write back   dear Mr Orlowski   and take me on. I'll be a star. Promise.

Lullaby for an Insomniac Princess

The queen was the first to suffer from insomnia; she found that she woke up in bed whenever she tried to turn over because her tummy, rounded and hard from the impending nativity of the princess, obstructed her lying on her stomach as she had done since she was a child. Her nurse laid her down in the cradle in that position 'so that in the future your deportment is all a lady's should be'. The queen's resulting wakefulness was haunted by fears for her baby; she tried to concentrate in the daytime on bright spring flowers, furry baby animals with all their parts in the right place, and other wholesome and gladdening forms; she tried to listen to harmonious, geometric music like Bach partitas, in order to keep her faculties calm and beautiful. But the world had a way of breaking in, with news flashes of abominations and catastrophes, of burnings, mutilations, famine, of bilharzia, typhoid, glaucoma and other diseases in kingdoms that seemed to grow nearer by the month. Furthermore, the FM signal for the classical music channel was so feeble or so intermittent and undependable that as she was trying to tune to it, she'd hit a raucous burst of youth rage on amplified electric guitar and cacophonous battery of drums. Then, in the night, she'd lie sleepless, thinking she had imprinted her child with the music's clangour; phantoms of its makers would steal into her bedroom and grimace triumphantly until she'd see her baby already body-pierced above, below, with yellowed teeth and stubbled skull.

The king was woken by the queen's restlessness. Sometimes she'd clutch him and even find terrors in such fantasies as, 'It'll look like a rabbit – I never should have looked at those bunnies and found them sweet!' Although he found it easier to lift himself into the sweet soft slow swing of sleep again, he tasted the white hours of the morning. 'It's training for the baby,' he joked.

But it wasn't a joke, because when their infant daughter was born, the land of sleep vanished altogether into deep mists of forgetfulness, became a foreign country they had never known; the Land of Nod no longer struck their tormented ears as a jocular, nursery phrase, but provoked longings as intense as doughnuts and chocolate éclairs during war shortages. How they dreamed, on their feet, of sleep.

They had help; the palace was filled with helpers, including a night nurse as well as a day nurse and several staff to wash the princess's tiny embroidered robes and bootees and iron the ribbons in her frilly bonnets. But the king and queen were late parents – she was forty-two when this, her first child was born, and he was seventy-three – and so they couldn't relinquish responsibility to hirelings, however carefully they had interviewed them, however searchingly they had called in references.

And then, as it turned out, the baby was an insomniac who outclassed her parents in wakefulness, who surpassed holy men and women who'd vowed to remain on their feet all the livelong day and night for the greater glory of God and his holy mother. She defeated the proven recipes of expert nurses, adepts of the wych hazel potion and the toddy of gin (in spite of those impeccable references), she defied the law of nature that lulls marching soldiers to sleep in the dead of winter and prostrates drivers at the wheel, pilots at the joystick and generals over their maps when in charge of a whole population's destiny. She was not acquainted with the need to sleep that weighs down the lids of lovers and husbands at crisis points of their lives, so that rather than argue the point, make the revelation, declare the passion and save the situation, they yawn and their heads drop and they start snoring. The baby, Imogen, did not hear the natural call of sleep.

The king and queen sent far and wide for remedies: they called in allopathic and homeopathic advice, they had teas blended and brewed from valerian and hops and poppy and verbena; they invited musicians to play at the child's bedside. The country was scoured for singers who knew a lullaby that the princess might not yet have heard; 'Hush-a-bye, baby', 'Softly shake the dreamland tree . . .', 'All the pretty little horses', were sung in the royal nursery in a dozen variations of lyric and tune, sometimes unaccompanied, sometimes not. But these soothing charms that had served for generations of children made no impression on little Imogen, lying, her lustrous, cerulean eyes wide-open with the slightly crazed look, already at the age of six months, of the inveterate insomniac.

When time-tested standards failed to take effect, the king and queen commissioned new lullabies from the most admired composers of the day, in their own realm and beyond. They came, with jew's harps and dulcimers, with wooden flutes and plangent violas, and played for Imogen. Poets were asked to write words to lull her; liquid syllables lilting to slow, slumbrous measures. But light-footed mimesis of prattle and babble, ditties and doggerel hummed and cooed, by voices that could enthral opera houses from Sydney to Paris, could not close the eyes of the new baby.

It wasn't that she cried; she did, sometimes, but no more than most infants struck with wind or sudden, nameless terror. But her perpetual vigilance was eerie, and it further upset her mother's already disrupted circadian rhythms; his child's arrhythmia affected the king's health, and the king's in turn touched the health of the kingdom ... *et ainsi de suite*, until the whole sky seemed filled with the brooding, wide-open eyes of the royal baby, staring and staring from some unique dimension of consciousness, until her wakefulness took possession of the inhabitants on the ground below like the chill shadow of a solar eclipse. Some inhabitants experienced the child's sleeplessness as a reproach on their own sloth: many calculated how much more intensively they would have lived if they had never slept, like her. A woman who has reached the age of sixty, it was whispered about, has spent probably more than twenty years asleep. What a waste of time – why couldn't everyone be more like Imogen?

When Imogen started to walk and to talk, her entire energies began to focus on the question: what happens when you sleep? She was consumed with longing, not to rest her weariness, for she had grown accustomed to its implacable presence in much the same way as a barefoot boy, crammed into boots to join the army, learns to live with the agony. But she longed to dream. Because she did not sleep, she needed company at all times, including during the small hours of the night, and so it turned out that by the time she was seven, she had the mental age of a fifteen-year-old, and, while tutors expired with tiredness over their lessons, she kept at her books. She read the Bible and *The Shepherd of Hermas* and the *Book of Enoch* and *The Divine Comedy* and *The Visions of the Daughters of Albion* and 'Goblin Market'; she pored over the profuse works of seers, of Hildegard of Bingen and Gertrude the Great and Hadewijk and Mechtild of Magdeburg and Christina the Astonishing. But communicating the experience of a dream is as elusive as using words to express the smell of crushed rue or roasting coffee. The inadequacy of language as an instrument of knowledge, Imogen learned, was not, however, the only problem regarding dreams. Everybody dreams according to his or her fashion: even Dante and Blake in all their eloquence could not tell Imogen what her own dreams would be.

So efforts redoubled to find a charm or a trick or a drug to bring sweet sleep to Imogen.

She collaborated with her teachers and helpers; her distraught parents spared no expense on the search. She communicated on the web with fellow sufferers from insomnia, she ordered rare copies of magical and medical treatises from antiquarian catalogues around the world, often competing with national libraries specialising in such materials. The Pierpont Morgan in New York, the Wellcome Institute in London, found themselves outbid. Many suggested methods failed, and some were too extreme to try: she did not want to hang by hooks through her nipples under the hypnosis of a holy man. Her hopes rose when her quest uncovered the existence of a rare mastic, recommended in a Yiddish Midrash on Paracelsus, and still in use in the Amazonian rainforest by a tribe that had only been discovered last year. But in vain. When the piece of chewing gum arrived, in a chemically sealed plastic sachet, and she put it eagerly in her mouth and began systematically working it round her teeth and tongue, she felt the usual dreaded response begin to tingle up her spine and the nape of her neck and fizz upwards to the crown of her head and the stalks of her eyes: wakefulness! This quarter ounce of aromatic ooze from an endangered tree had cost, if you threw in the price of the air freight, more than a diamond the same size; and it had affected Imogen like strong peppermint, straight up her nose to rekindle that spot in her brain that never let her sleep: her completely dysfunctional hypothalamus, her squinting pineal eye, her burst Cartesian soul-seat, the perverse fountainhead of her entirely ill-assorted, awry, unnatural circadian rhythms.

One day, a fowler called at the palace and asked to see the insomniac princess: he had a story to tell her that might help her problem. She had him let into her study. He was red-haired and freckled, and wore over his jeans and sneakers a tattercoat of browns and greens and blacks. 'Camouflage in the woods,' he said. He set down a cage. He had made it, he told her, from a wine carton and some wire mesh. Though he bore a faint resemblance to Papageno, his cage was empty. But he did use it to trap songbirds, he said.

Imogen was shocked. She almost seized the clumsy object then and there and would have him clap't in irons if she'd been a princess in that kind of story. But he shushed her with a finger to his lips, and set the cage down on the floor behind him, out of reach.

He said to her, 'It's a poor thing, made in the image of the bird it could house: a poor, brown, dull bird that flutters from branch to branch in twilight, singing out in profound, unspeakable sorrow.'

'But it's against the law to trap songbirds,' said Imogen. 'And unless you're able to give me a full explanation of what you think you're up to, I'll report you and have you arrested for crimes against wildlife.' Though her biological age was still only eight, and she inhabited a child's body, she had acquired the manners and speech of an adult through her long years awake. 'Besides, even though I'm suffer-ing from chronic insomnia, I'm perfectly able to cope, and I'm certainly not going to resort to crime to cure myself.'

He waved away her protests, and smiled and took out a penny whistle and played a tune on it, which trilled and flowed and curled and warbled till her heart beat faster and her breath quickened. 'You recognise that, I'm sure?'

'It's a nightingale – I suppose,' she said, a little crossly. 'I've heard recordings hundreds of times, though we don't have any around here any more – no doubt because of people like you.'

'Yes, it's a nightingale – the male of the species.' Then he smiled again, and put the pipe to his mouth again, and again she felt the trembly feelings in her legs and in her chest and she wanted to put out her hands to catch the notes. 'But in all the stories, it's not the male who sings, but the female – she's the one who knows the true nature of joy. And of sorrow. Her song makes the male bird's sound like cold chisels hammering at stone or saucepans bashed together under the bride and groom's window in the charivari of oldentime.'

'What do you mean?' cried Imogen. 'What does her song sound like?'

'Nobody knows – it's only been described by others – by Ovid that miserable complainer, and by poor mad John Clare and by Keats, who knew he was dying when he heard it and by one or two others. But what they found to say can't match the first-hand experience.' He paused, and looked at her intently with his greeny-brown eyes in his flecked skin with his head cocked to one side, and he blew a warbling cascando through his pipe. 'But I know where to find her – and if you don't want me to trap her to bring her here, I can take you there.'

Imogen had read Keats's Ode and knew some of its most famous lines by heart, including the bit about forgetting 'the weariness, the fever, and the fret, / Here where men sit and hear each other groan . . .', and she identified strongly with the poet because her insomnia made her very pale and thin and indeed, even spectral. She knew about Philomel having her tongue cut out by her lustful brother-in-law Tereus, because she'd been reading classics since she was a toddler, however much rape, incest and child-murder and nasty violence they contained. She knew that Philomel's dumbness was turned into the nightingale's enchanted eloquence and music – the female nightingale's pouring forth in such an ecstasy. And as her visitor, in his tattercoat like bedraggled wings, played some more on his pipe, she wanted to hear the song that was even more enthralling than this one.

'I'll come with you, as long as you promise not to bring that cage or hurt the bird – if you can find her as you seem to think you can.'

The king and queen were aghast that Imogen insisted on leaving with this itinerant, this tatterdemalion, who had turned up and had no background or reputation, let alone any references. Although they wrung their hands and equipped her with a pager – there was no point giving her a mobile phone, the fowler pointed out, as there wouldn't be anywhere to recharge it in the wildwood where they were headed – Imogen's parents were secretly hoping that in her absence, the glare of her vigilance might fade from their minds and they might themselves have a good night's rest.

The fowler sprang ahead into the woods; Imogen kept up with him as best she could, but his figure was difficult to pick out against the foliage, especially in the thickest parts, where the canopy of the trees created shadows, but also in the gaps, in the dapple of perpendicular sunlight. She called out to him to slow down, and he turned and smiled so she saw the gleam on his teeth and the light dancing in his bright eyes.

'Come on, my little princess!' he called. 'We must reach the heart of the heart of the wildwood before nightfall and set up our camp so that we can hear her when she starts to sing.'

Imogen stumbled on behind him; the jeans from Junior Gaultier she'd put on for the expedition were too stylishly cut for comfort and the sneaker's laces on her left foot had come undone. But she was afraid that if she stopped to tie them, she'd lose sight of her guide, who seemed to move so lightly through the trees that he trod on air.

'Stop!' she cried out, and again he turned but beckoned to her with one pinnate arm outstretched and she flung herself on; her legs were feeling thick and heavy and her heart was thumping with the unaccustomed effort. It was becoming harder and harder to pick up her feet and avoid the mesh of roots and brambles and undergrowth that offered him no obstacle but clutched at her with hooked fingers.

Imogen, the little princess, was scared.

The light under the wildwood branches was patchy and the ground, where it fell in shapes like the ciphers of some language she had never studied, seemed to be rising up to impede her.

Again, she cried out to him.

But this time, there was no answer.

She stopped, and the sound of her own breathing terrified her – like some trapped animal, squealing. Then she realised it was her own voice and she stifled herself to listen out.

Heaving and creaking of branches, snapping of twigs and scattering of leaves – was that the fowler?

Faintly, she heard him call her, 'Im—o—gen! Im—o—gen! This way!'

She tried to plunge on, but her limbs wouldn't obey her. She dropped down where she was, and the mulch was cool and soft. She lay there till she could hear past her beating heart and harshly taken breath and sift the sounds of the wildwood; gradually the noises regrouped themselves, fell into patterns, subsided and settled.

Then she heard the song: and when she woke, she was in her bed, there were tears on her cheeks and it was two o'clock in the afternoon.

'You've slept – for hours!' said her mother, leaning in to kiss her. 'We were so worried for you. It's stupid, but it was such a shock.'

'But so happy, too,' said her father.

'I had a dream,' said Imogen, 'and I was just about to hear the most wonderful music in the world . . . But then I woke up.' And she laughed, and turned over on the pillow and closed her eyes. 'Maybe if I go to sleep again, I'll hear some more.'

Stone Girl

1

Tessa was in the passage, kitted out in the new boots from the farmers' Cash & Carry, where Hugh had taken her to buy a pair of waterproof lace-ups – and some socks; till then, she'd only had footwear fit for parquet and carpets. He opened a map of the moor to show her where they'd be going; the pale, whorled expanse of open ground was sprinkled with Gothic ciphers marking the position of standing stones and circles; near them capitals in red spelled out the dangers of the terrain – swamps and bogs that could swallow a motorbike with a single satisfied burp. As once happened, he told her, to a friend out scrambling. Snowdrifts in winter, swollen streams in spring, and glinting granite scarps: it wasn't polite land, Hugh informed Tessa with some pride, his finger pointing at one of the sites, the 'Nine Maidens'.

When Hugh began taking Tessa walking on the moor, her ideas of pastoral had to change. There were sheep, but they weren't placid. As they approached a flock down a bridle path, on the other side of a stout drystone wall, the animals would suddenly take fright; they'd career clumsily across the fields, their terror increasing if the sun went behind a cloud and the shadow, whipped by the breeze, began to give chase. The lambs would cry out where they'd been left behind and soon the field was in turmoil. Hugh and Tessa stood together by the wall and watched as the young cried piteously for their ewes, and then picking up the right pitch and cadence of the bleating, rushed to shelter by their mams' side again.

'There's a language,' she said, 'with a word for home that's made up from the words for a ewe and her lamb.'

Hugh was offering her a home. It had been mostly rented rooms for her before, in her student days. She was anxious, though, about his house on the moor. She couldn't help the scratchy, scared jumpiness she felt in the house that he'd lived in before they knew each other, that he'd shared with Sophie. Sophie and he had chosen it, they'd moved in together, they'd been married in it.

But he gave Tessa a room of her own, the one upstairs with a view of the moor. He brought offerings, to the house, to the room, with messages and crosses marked for kisses. He emptied cupboards and made room on shelves, tidied spaces and plumped cushions, he found pictures for the walls and jokes and posters, he swept and dusted, he covered the tracks of the last years. By nature he was thorough and quick and efficient, she could see that, and he went over the house with care, so that there were none of the traces she was afraid of: no stains on the mattress, no hair in the plughole, no nail varnish on a window sill, no earring under the bed, no tampax in the bathroom cupboard.

When she looked at the moor from the back of the house, she could see the broken walls of the highest field, long ago abandoned. When the land was given away in some gesture towards ending feudalism, settlers had struggled to farm there, but it wasn't possible: it was stony soil, and it threatened to turn everything into its own likeness. Huge boulders had been hauled here to stand on end, and dug in, set up in rings and lines a very long time ago. They couldn't pick them out on the moor from the house, though some of the locals who gathered in the pub said they could from other points in the village.

That day, when they took the Ordnance Survey map to try and find the Nine Maidens, the stones weren't there, not where they were marked. In the pub, a professional hiker said they'd simply missed them, it wasn't hard to do. Another consoled them, 'The moor turns you around. No landmarks, just vistas of cloud, coming to the boil over the horizon!' But Hugh was gloomy about it; it was like missing a cathedral, he said, and he wanted, after several years in the area, to show he recognised its landscape like his own bones.

Nobody knew what these rocks meant – were they really places of worship – of sacrifice? Were they tombs? They were cult sites now, certainly, attracting ley line theorists, goddess devotees, green man followers. They bred all kinds of cautionary tales, repeated over the pints: you can never count the stones, some said. Every time you'd start again, one of the stones would have moved and there'd be more of them, or fewer of them than you'd thought and you had to start again.

The petrified bodies of dancing girls made up the ring – though again, the number shifted. They'd been out carousing one Saturday night on the high hump of the moor by moonlight and had forgotten the hour. When the next day dawned, and they were still dancing, even though they'd given their word, divine providence struck. It was His day they were defiling, so, looming suddenly, the Lord set His jaw and beetled His brows and rolled His eyes and terrorised them into stone.

Did they die, in their new state? Or did life lurk inside the stones and spark them into dancing again, some nights under the moon? The question wasn't settled; the girls were still unburied, their spirits roaming. They'd be too old – far too tough – laughed Tessa's informants, for the appetites of the ogre with iron teeth who stalked bad children and stowed them in his haversack, who tied its mouth with an old bootlace and carried them off to hell like squirming ferrets to put them in a coop in his lair on the moor and fatten for his table. Nor would the demon huntsman who haunted the moor fancy them for his supper: he'd once thrown down a game pouch from his horse at a wayfarer who asked him, passing the time of day, if he'd enjoyed good sport. The huntsman crowed as he made the gift, and when the hungry traveller opened the bag he found his baby in it, dead.

One cold afternoon later that summer, when they weren't looking for the Maidens, Hugh and Tessa came across them;

an easterly breeze was cutting up there on the ridge of the moor, and they crouched under the lea of one of the tallest stones, to find shelter. Hugh had brought a rucksack with a flask of tea and some chocolate. The heat and the sugar refreshed their energies, but it was true that it was hard to number the mute, chill maidens. It seemed to Tessa as if there was always one more, on the edge of her vision; one who was still moving, trying to struggle free from providence's Gorgon stare. It was a harsh place: she couldn't even see it in colour, but only in flinty grey and black, like the dust fields of a sunless underworld.

2

'No, don't pull away from me. If you want to learn, you must let me hold you. Close.'

Her mother lifted Tessa at the waist, drew her tightly into her body. The 'Six Five Special' was humming from the telly; Mrs Foxton had been buffing her nails as her daughter watched. But when Tessa began jigging around, Hedy Foxton put away her manicure set in its red morocco case, and stood up and took the twelve-year-old by the hands and begun pushing and pulling her to make her feet move to the rhythm. Tessa let her arms shunt in and out to her mother's prompts, and for the hundredth time, felt the weight of her flesh bother the beautiful willowy woman who was Hedy Foxton, and who was at that moment shaking her shoulders in a shimmy and stepping intricately this way and that. Mr Foxton, sitting in his armchair by the gas fire, looked over the top of his paper and tipped his glasses back straight to look at them, then thumped the paper with one fist, lightly, and rolled his eyes.

'Is there to be no peace in this house of women?' At that, her mother picked Tessa up, giving him a quick flash of a smile, and set her on top of her feet, clasping her tightly so that she couldn't do otherwise than move with her.

'A little elephant, our Tessa,' her father always said.

But soon, the music and Hedy's movements began to overcome her resistance, and she let her mother lead, her feet in their school brown strap shoes plumped on top of her mother's navy blue court heels and 15 denier stockings; she was trying to keep herself light, not to ladder them or weigh down on her toes. Soon they were swaying and turning together, and Hedy Foxton was laughing with pleasure.

'See, you're getting the hang of it now – always yield to your partner – that's the secret of it.' She paused; all of a sudden, she was serious. 'Though God knows, not many men know how to dance.'

For the party the Foxtons held that summer, Tessa was allowed her first pair of grown-up shoes. Dolcis in the High Street dyed them to match her dress. Satin pumps with three-inch heels. She had turned thirteen, and had to bend her legs at the knee to walk in them without tottering, which made her head dip and bob in rhythm, like a stilt at the water's edge on the beach. Hedy made her a dress without a pattern, from a picture in *Vogue*: it was nylon organza in shocking pink, over an underskirt of lighter-coloured, moiré taffeta which created shimmering effects; she sewed floating panels from the shoulders which could be wafted as one danced. She showed her daughter how.

'Mine are Californian cowhide,' said the family friend. He'd just done military service, and his brogues were very shiny. This was Cambridge in the late fifties, and he was all promise, a Rupert Brooke, a Lytton Strachey. He lifted Tessa to stand on his gleaming toecaps to dance and she first tasted the disappointments of the heart when, a few months later, she learned how foolish her love for him was.

'You dodo,' said Jem, who had spots and was a poet. 'He's your mother's boyfriend. Everyone knows that.'

3

When Good King Wenceslas invited the page to tread in his footsteps, did it mean that they had special powers? After all, Tessa thought, the page could have shuffled along in the wake of his master, and he wouldn't have got lost, so why did he have to struggle to put his feet down in the exact same place, like a child avoiding the lions and the bears who lurk under the paving stones? And those holes in the snow, where the page stepped so carefully, were they still crisply shaped to the soles of Wenceslas's top boots, or were they already soft pits, melted by the warmth of the good king's body?

At Christmas, singing the carol in Hugh's village church where he had wanted her to come with him, Tessa imagined Wenceslas had electric boots. When the page put his foot down in the tracks the good king had made, each step became a bed, a lap, a breast. Otherwise he would have turned as cold and immobile as the stone girls on the moor. The footsteps brought him back to life from the cold. She put her hand in Hugh's but he didn't squeeze it back; it wasn't right in church.

4

Tessa's first boyfriend, her partner at college, took photographs of her, all over, every bit of her and made a collage, which he stuck on a board by his desk. He included her feet at first, but looking at the print, decided they didn't fit the rest of her, they were wrong. She realised then that she had never liked her feet either, and thinking of standing on them made her feel dizzy. How did they manage to hold up the whole of the rest of her, the whole bulk and weight of her with that heavy head on top of it all? Perhaps they weren't more unwieldly than average, but they were still ill-fitting tools, and she longed for those almond slivers on which Cinderella floated and flitted.

The bigness happened when Tessa wasn't yet fully grown; her feet made her look like a puppy whose size has out-stripped its acquired powers of coordination and so it trips and slithers and sprawls, limbs tangled up in themselves. She wasn't self-conscious about it, then, but after that first party of her parents' when she was allowed to stay up, she took to wearing stilettos after school and during the holidays, because she liked the way the pointed ends trimmed her feet into neat palette knives. They also bunched up her toes till they crossed and warped; and walking on the moor, her new boots pinched her displaced knuckles even through the hiking socks.

One afternoon that summer with Hugh, when Tessa was on her way to the library in the nearby town, she passed a new aromatherapy parlour; it was called, You Shall Go To The Ball, according to a board out on the pavement, in swirly writing amid a shower of glitter, and a painting of a Hindu love goddess with purple-black hair, one leg bent up behind the other and a set of pretty crimson-painted toes. A customer was in a chair with a copy of *Dazed & Confused*; when the beautician who was bending over her caught sight of Tessa hovering, she beckoned through the doorway. She had a newly hatched chick haircut and a silver ring through her left nostril; Tessa waved and called back,

'Another time – maybe when my mum's coming to stay.' But the girl waved again, commandingly, 'Aw, go on, treat yourself.' With a sidelong flicker and closing of her eyes, let's pretend bliss, she said, 'We're nearly done here. Have a foot massage, go on.'

Tessa, magnetised, drifted towards her.

An acupuncture chart was framed on the wall, with a close-up diagram of the soles of the foot with the pressure points linked up to the ventricles of the heart and sections of the brain. Inside, a pervasive roseate cloud of scented oils wrapped her, pierced with prickles of pepper and mint and allspice. She thought, maybe this is the formula that would make all feet feel as if they've slipped easily into Cinderella's lost slipper.

The beautician's name was Kira; it had been revealed to her on a weekend course she'd taken to find the woman inside her. She was very relieved, because she'd never felt like the name she was born with, Maureen, or so she began telling Tessa, as she filed her feet, vigorously flexing a large emery board over the hard skin till it fell off in grey flakes onto the towel.

'In ancient China, they used to call them lotus feet,' she was saying, 'but they didn't smell anything like lotus. No, they didn't come up roses. When they took the bandages off, they stank. The flesh underneath all rotted and black and manky. That's Chinese foot-binding for you. It was all for show. And they had thirty-two ways of walking, isn't that amazing? Cinderella didn't have to do that, she just had to have little feet.' Kira giggled, as she took Tessa's foot firmly and placed it in a hot tub of frothy aromatic water. 'Just keep them there, to soften up the cuticles. They had to learn all those different walks, right, one for getting his tea, one for running his bath, one for going to bed.' She put the other foot now to join its fellow in the basin. 'Ten minutes.' She looked at Tessa's immersed feet with satisfaction. 'Then it's the best part. We have to work on the inner you.'

Tessa sat quietly, thinking of a Chinese woman keeping on her shoes in bed so that the man wouldn't catch a whiff of that rottenness. But real erotic appetite didn't flinch at smells of mortality, did it? No foot fetishist minded what a foot, delivered from its shell, from its sheath, looked like. This is what Tessa couldn't stretch her mind to grasp – or rather, her senses – and she suspected this failure revealed a deficit in her, of libido, of the ability to engage with another, with his flesh, with Hugh's smells and bumps and sheddings. I've swum into the mirror, she thought, where all is smooth and glassy and odourless, the coated paper of fashion plates. Kira, wreathed in a stupor of rose petals and violets and musk oils, doesn't know the half of it for the rest of us. She remembered her mother, turning over the pages of the glossies and homing in on the imperfections of the most dazzling stars.

It was a stroke of inspiration, that fairy-tale glass for Cinderella's slipper. The Ugly Sisters didn't have to cut off their heels and cut off their toes to shove their big plates into the slipper in the prince's hand. It was the shoe's edges that sliced off the offending parts. 'Turn and peep, Turn and peep, There's blood within the shoe.'

Tessa said to Kira, 'I heard on the radio that Cinderella's

glass slipper was really made of fur after all, did you know that?'

Yes, thought Tessa, that's what I'd like: dancing shoes as soft as fleece.

Kira came back and lifted Tessa's feet out of the basin, which was tepid now, and placed one in her lap on a towel and began applying herself to the nails with a pair of tiny scissors and an orange stick.

Nodding towards a trolley behind her, she told Tessa, 'Bring it closer and choose your colour – the new Graffiti polishes, they're wicked.' She was cradling her feet in her lap and pressing them between strong fingers and thumbs. 'This is the best bit.' She closed her eyes, and this time her blissed-out look no longer seemed an act. 'I'm finding all those toxins and letting them go.'

'Frosted anthracite,' said Tessa.

5

The long slow gradient of the moor out of Tessa's window changed under the light; in a single day it could lour very close and damp, then clear all of a sudden and sail away to the horizon, wide and far and dreamy. Though it kept itself to itself, the land had been worn in, worked to the hand and the foot, walked, rubbed down, like old stone treads sagging under millions of ghost footsteps, and the rocks on the moor humped to the movement of the wind. Sometimes, when she was looking out of the window, the stone looked cast to a mould by those who had passed by and trodden it. Like Hugh's jeans, when he'd thrown them off before coming to bed.

Sophie had left her shape there, too, in the pair of gardening gloves that lay with still fingers bent as if grasping at the air. Tessa had come across them in the trug with the masonry nails and the training wire and the secateurs. She put them on and moved through the garden, bending over the plants and pulling up fistfuls of herb robert and buttercup that were choking the new roses she'd planted.

Husbandry was a funny word for the work of making a home, she thought. Living here on the moor, it kept coming to mind; it implied vigilance and repair, walking the rows to inspect each plant, tying back a new shoot here, lodging a loose stone back in the wall there, tracking the relation of land and inhabitant, in order to take up occupation of the space in your turn.

What was the phrase, fits like an old shoe? And that footprint in the dust on the moon, corrugated, splay: the unmistakable – and indelible – sign of human presence.

Tessa was inhabiting the already inhabited, fitting herself to the existing shape of things, finding the old paths to follow. The shapes were already there when she moved in with Hugh. She'd taken a step, across his threshold, to tread in the hollows of his footprints. Her new boots, those stout lace-ups for the moor, were now standing in the passage beside Hugh's; after going out for a walk, they'd fall sideways together, unlaced, an old hedge laid down after the summer, branches intertwined. Tessa could hear his footfalls below her room as he left his study for the kitchen to make some tea.

She thought then, I am the stone girl missing from the ring, the one who wasn't in the count when I tried to number the stones.

Murderers I Have Known

Murder is moving in next door. I don't mean street gangs or bomb factories in suburban kitchens; I mean the best addresses, official receptions, dinner parties. People seem to think that thrillers are escapist, that films about rape, massacres and mayhem merely offer fantasy pap. Of course, some of the murderers I've met recently aren't really murderers, they're just acting the part, or being paid to make-believe. But the number of would-be real ones I'm encountering is on the increase, and they're not as furtive about it as they must have been in the past, when you didn't find yourself sitting next to one at dinner as if it were the most routine thing in the world. Murder's becoming naturalised, an import into the social landscape that feels as if it belongs there, like those garden escapes that begin by adding an exotic touch to a railway siding or a dilapidated parapet and end up looking plain weed-like: overgrown patches of Himalayan balsam, clumps of purple buddleia. Last month, I came across no less than two bona fide murderers. In one week.

Before that, over the whole of the last twenty years, I'd only known two others all told – in real life, I mean – and doubling the score like that all of a sudden in one week has made me wonder. I know one shouldn't put faith in signs or portents, and I'm sceptical on the whole about numerology and astrology and most of the other New Age pseudo-sciences. But we are living in the degenerate moment of the century, and ancient wisdom shouldn't really be judged on its present showing. The artists that mean the most to me, the ones I've studied and continued to study, were all deeply involved in the relation between the natural and the supernatural, they discovered patterns and systems everywhere and reproduced them in their work, in the geometry of their compositions, in the plan of their buildings. Chance itself belongs to the grand design. So I thought I should be on the alert. In case.

I'm going to take my murderers one by one, working backwards.

I was invited to a charity gala at the embassy where my ex-stepmother Natalia works. She gave me a ticket (they were around £50 each – for Bosnian relief). Her embassy occupies one of those great London houses with nymphs in white plaster looking frisky on pale green walls and festoons in the cornices; the effect is a bit marred by the twitching of the cream plastic alarm sensors fixed in each corner of the room up among the acanthus spikes. We sat down to listen to the recital on gilt lyre-backed chairs with crimson brocade-cushioned seats – a young pianist, winner of some recent, international competition was playing; between her pieces, an acting duo would be performing works by great national poets.

Natalia was excited: she'd helped select the readings. She also has a new lover, and he was there. It's odd seeing a man in a black tie when all you've heard about him is how hot he is. I looked at his narrow head, along the row from where I was sitting, at the smooth planes of his skull under longish grey hair, with just a hint of a curl, at the urbane composure of his mouth as he attended to the music. I thought of the same face grimacing in the throes of thrusting into Natalia and I had to bite my lip. To stop myself giggling. Which wouldn't have been appropriate at all, as the pianist had begun the Chopin, and was playing it in a rather dark, dry style, very unlike the moonlit swooning stuff I'm more used to. She had thin, tough little arms, and darted at the keys, so that in her green moiré décolleté dress she looked like a hummingbird poking at the keyboard to extract wild honey.

I had to quell my mental pictures of Natalia when she was married to my father, too. It didn't last long, and he's dead now, but we became good friends at the time; she's only twelve years older than me, and she was a wonderfully conspiratorial stepmother, full of secret treats for a child, and willing to share grown-up knowledge later with the avid teenager I became. And she was an ally, too, when it mattered. Of course, I had to keep a difficult balance between her and Mum, who in one way was glad to be rid of Dad but didn't want to lose me into the bargain.

But I could talk to Natalia – and still can – about things I could never bring up with my real mother; whether fellatio cheapens you, for instance. We got on, we joined forces; I think Dad felt rather threatened by us, in fact, and I have to admit it gave me a tingle to listen to Natalia's worldly wisdom and to imagine her in bed with my father.

There was a glittering crowd at the embassy, as a gossip columnist would say, and they paid attention to the concert, making a fairly good job of keeping still, which was just as well, as so many encrusted textiles, hand-sewn with beads and pearls, had gone into the parrot-motley on display that if any of the audience had moved they would have provided involuntary percussion. Natalia looked along the row and caught my eye; we exchanged smiles – she was making sure I was glad to be there, and I was.

The pianist took a bow; she was lightly flushed now, and her startled eyes softened as she accepted the applause. The waiters passed with champagne and we toasted her where she stood on the rostrum imported into the salon for the occasion.

The English actor then took the stage; he explained that he would be translating each poem in turn. The cele-brated actress appeared, furled in striped Lycra like a golfing umbrella. 'Versace,' whispered several voices as the actor asked for a hand to welcome her. We sipped as she began.

Her style was old school: she reminded me of paintings of Garrick striking attitudes of rage and despair. She had picked for us that night, she said, after her first poem, a lovers' bouquet – flowers of passion, flowers of the night. She went on, throwing out an arm, bulging her eyes, swelling her throat – which flowed smoothly into the rise and fall of her breast so that I understood why 'throat' is used when breasts are meant in so many nineteenth-century precursors of the bodice-ripper. She was intoning:

'*Verrà la morte*
Ed avrà i tuoi occhi.'

Sotto voce, the Englishman translated:

'Death will come
And she will have your eyes.'

The poem had been written by a man, a famous suicide, and we were hushed by his momentary presence. Like a flash from an areoplane's wings as it catches the sun, he flickered for an instant across the room, alive again. Love and death, the *femme fatale*; the women in the audience lowered their own eyes modestly, accepting the tribute with decorum.

Afterwards, I met the first murderer. He was handsome, I suppose, in a narcissistic way, and his name was familiar. I remarked on this, and he snapped, 'You've probably read about me. It was a nightmare from beginning to end, your vampire press drank my blood. I still haven't recovered.'

He'd been charged with attempted murder – I have to admit I'm being unfair when I dub him a murderer as he didn't manage to do it – and besides, I should register his protest at the time and ever since that he never intended to kill his girlfriend, that it was a completely blunt knife, that he was a fool but not a criminal, that it was all a misunderstanding arising from the natural, manly jealousy of men from his country which, she, an Englishwoman, had not come across before, that she had dropped the charges because she realised he wasn't in earnest and that she should never have called the police, etc., etc.

Natalia had overseen the *placement*. Afterwards, she came up to me and whispered, 'Someone switched him – I'd put you between two real winners. Come and sit here now, with us. That man's become such a bore about that whole business. I'm sorry.' She took my hand and led me to sit down next to her new lover.

We were awkward with each other; I think men often are with their lover's girlfriends. We're like parish priests, privy to the secrets of the confessional, and the main root of feeling against the church isn't anything high-minded like caring about teenage mothers, but sexual insecurity – the priests get to hear all about the men from the women and then they give advice – 'He wanted you to do that, did he? What a monster! Well, if he tries that again, don't go along with it.' Naturally men don't like it. Well, in more secular societies, like London today and the embassy circuit, I looked like I might be playing father confessor to Natalia, and Louis was wary. He was a bit of a smoothie, too, and that in turn put me on my guard. 'So, is the international art world coping?' he asked me. 'Or are even Old Masters vulnerable to recession?' I told him I was still travelling a great deal, couriering pictures from one show to another. He showed some interest – he was in insurance – and I told him about my recent trip to Tokyo with one of the gallery's Guercino drawings.

As I got entangled in the story, I realised, More murder, but at least this one's safe inside a cherrywood frame, and happened a long time ago. The drawing shows the revenge of Absalom on his brother Amnon after Amnon has tricked Tamar their sister into his bedroom by pretending to be ill. She goes in to give him food, and he assaults her. And discards her brutally, afterwards. Louis asked me, 'Was Guercino that low-life character, the one they made the film about?' 'No,' I said quickly, 'he's not Caravaggio. He didn't do anything criminal himself, as far as I know.'

I actually loved the drawing I'd carried to the other side of the world and would be collecting it again, in two months' time, to return to Prints and Drawings. Guercino had drawn the incident like a tavern brawl, as if the remote Old Testament episode was unfolding at the table next to him. The hired assassins were in seventeenth-century clothes, and the stilettos they raised against Amnon could have been bought from any cutler in Bologna at the time. But what I liked was that Guercino wasn't struggling to capture the violence of the incident by lingering on gouts of blood or raw flesh like so many religious artists. He was striving, with his stabs and dashes of ink, to catch the feelings of the murderers and their victim: he's an artist who's interested in what's going on inside someone's head.

'*Plus ça change*,' said Louis, when I'd scrambled to the

end of my account. 'But it is difficult to think of sublime Old Masters leading such squalid lives.'

The next day the would-be-murderer-who-wasn't sent me a press dossier he'd compiled as part of his attempt at vindication. I didn't read it all, but as I skimmed, I saw it contained terrible tales of life in prison, where he'd spent a few months until the case came to a hearing and his erstwhile beloved dropped her charges. He was a wronged man, I could see that. He also suggested we have lunch together.

I couldn't help asking myself what does the poet do after he has thought/said/written, 'Death will come/And will have your eyes.' If he doesn't kill himself, what is the logical next act for the man who sees death in the face of the woman he loves – or thinks he loves – as so many of the lovers and poets and other men of genius we revere said they did?

Natalia was telling me a bit more about her new man, Louis, over a plate of pasta in a restaurant near the gallery. I was becoming more and more uneasy, and, as I did so, I had to keep my features shellacked with a brave, complicit smile. I was afraid: one, that Louis was far too good to be true; two, that I suspected him only because I was jealous.

Recently, I've been in retreat from sex; I've never got used to having sex without strong feelings coming into play. When I'm travelling for the museum, most of the opportunities I get are necessarily casual and I'm pretty stiff with them. Natalia doesn't agree with me about this – one of the reasons we're still such friends is that she's bold and pleasure-loving and she's always encouraging me, in a maternal fashion, to be a little bit less inhibited, to lead through my strengths, have more confidence, overcome my innate anhedonia – the condition I share with Woody Allen, though it turns out he doesn't suffer from it to quite the same paralytic degree as I do. So in one sense, I did believe in Natalia's passion and its reciprocation; I was being a crabbed old killjoy, as usual, when I felt doubts breaking up my smiling face as I swallowed the last mouthfuls of *linguine alla boscaiola*.

At the same time as I struggled with these contradictions, I also began to feel protective towards Natalia – she was lost in her illusions, Louis would turn out no better than my father, and she'd suffer, and it would be ghastly for everyone. I suddenly realised that ever since Louis came into her life, she's had a cough and it isn't going away. She's not a smoker, and the suspicion floated into my mind and went on glinting there that Louis might be poisoning her bit by bit. What for? Well, the pleasure of revenge. Time for a reckoning – Death will come and she will have your eyes – that kind of thing. Get in first, before the other has a chance to deal the deathblow. At the same time, I knew I was being absurd. I was clearly becoming a timorous old spinster; lack of sex was driving me a bit bonkers, and I'd soon be twitching the lace curtains (slatted natural linen blinds, in fact) on my front window before opening the front door to the postman.

Then I went to a new play which had had good notices – I could only get tickets for the matinée, so it was a Saturday afternoon. Richard Nelson's *Two Shakespearean Actors*. It was entertaining stuff, about Charles Macready and Edwin Forrest, the rival interpreters of the Bard in the early nineteenth century, and it gave two performers an opportunity to parody Victorian acting styles. Which they seized with gusto – John Carlisle, who's a statuesque fellow, was playing Macready, and he made the Italian diva of the charity gala look austere by comparison as he used his splendid proportions (mighty knees, mighty profile) to advantage, striding and flinging arms and legs akimbo to accompany the florid cadenzas of his soliloquies. The American Edwin Forrest was meant to be a precursor of the Stanislavski school, so Anton Lesser played the part with Brando mumbles and James Dean adolescent hangdog head-lolling, curled in on himself and whispering from the heart in the intensity of emotion. (In fact, theatre pictures suggest the opposite, in terms of history: Macready did away with ranting, introduced introspective, faithful readings of the original texts, while it was Forrest who continued, on the boards of Broadway, the full-blooded meaty mode of declamation.)

Naturally, Macbeth wasn't the two rivals' only great role. Forrest, in particular, made his name with one of the all-time tearjerkers, *Metamora, or the Last of the Wampanoags*, 'the best and almost the sole survivor of the sixty-odd Indian dramas of the period', the programme informed us. This inflamed piece climaxes when the Indian chief Metamora kills his beloved wife rather than let her fall into the hands of the white man and become his slave. He then commits suicide over her dead body. She never speaks at all in the scene – it was a vehicle for Forrest after all, who had commissioned the play specially to star in. And the actress's tragic looks were eloquent enough. Tears filled her ox eyes under the beaded headband and rolled down her lovely Minnehaha-Laughing Water cheeks as Metamora readied himself – and her – for the *coup de grâce*. His weapon was a dagger, too.

Macready's other crowd-puller was *Othello* – and so we were treated to that fatal scene as well. A cushion, this time, of course.

In spite of my anxieties about Natalia and about Louis, I didn't immediately connect the play with my life in any way at all, until the friend I was with that afternoon nudged me, as we were eating our ice creams in the interval, and I looked up across the foyer and saw . . . the most famous recent murderer of all, familiar from a hundred front pages, the one who's meant to have killed his girlfriend but the trial was thrown out after some kind of wrong size glove cock-up, that kind of technicality, a mega-rich businessman with a chain of gyms and other interests, who then sold his story to a writer, and then to a film producer, and the girlfriend was played by a newcomer from Wales who won an Oscar and cried on the podium that she felt she was in spiritual communication with the dead girlfriend, and so on and so forth, until the whole incident made everyone involved lots more money than even they had started with.

However, we weren't completely sure it was him. Partly

because I really didn't want it to be him; it seemed a bad omen, though, as I say, I try and resist what I think of as empty contemporary fatalism. But I'm afraid it was. He was with a blonde, my age, in chic, European clothes; they weren't speaking much. I found I couldn't stop glancing over to look at him; when I was studying portraits, the lecturers would project a painting, by Titian or by Van Eyck, and say, 'Look, how the artist has caught the character of the man in his face or in his stance, or in the way he clasps his hands.' I wanted to find a sign of what this man, so recently on trial for murder, had done. I wanted to see it in his expression, or in his hands. I wanted it to show.

I really knew the first murderer I ever met. He was the rapist who terrorised a whole county for three years and came to be known as The Sussex Strangler. When he was finally caught, on his bike in the small hours, clad from head to toe in rubber gear with a clothes line in the saddlebag, he turned out to be John Thompson, the odd-job man who used to come round and ask for work at the house where Dad and Natalia moved to after they got married. It was in the country, near Lewes. I'd known him for nine years of my life, and I'd often been alone with him at home while Natalia and Dad went out – there are a lot of parties in Sussex, if you like socialising, which they did. Sometimes, he'd watch the telly for ten minutes or so with me, before going back to raking out a drain or rawl-plugging some fallen kitchen shelving for Natalia.

He was a small but stringy man, and a bit of a joker. Once, he'd been asked to clear the climbing roses out of the gutters along the edge of the roof, and he was up on a ladder against the house, and the briars were dropping to the ground below as he clipped them with the secateurs. It was an Indian summer afternoon, and it must have been the weekend, as I was sitting on the lawn with a book and Natalia had rolled up the cap sleeves on her T-shirt to tan her arms. Then Johnnie, as Natalia called him, began chucking the briars about and one or two of them fell beside us, grazing us as they fell.

'Watch out, Johnnie,' Natalia called out. 'You're hitting us with the rose cuttings.'

He laughed merrily – and playfully aimed a rose branch like a paper dart and we had to duck to prevent it doing us damage – so Natalia at that point got furious, and ordered him to stop it instantly. He did so, sniggering.

At the time, it seemed silly stuff, rather than seriously menacing behaviour.

He was a prankster, too, when he was committing his crimes. He'd jump through the window of a room in a nurses' hostel whooping like a Red Indian with 'Elvis is King' or 'Sympathy for the Devil' scrawled in gold Pentel on the crotch of his rubber outfit. But he used the clothes line and he nearly killed one of his victims, his fourteenth rape I think it was, when she fought him.

Again, I realise I'm being casual with the truth – the Sussex Strangler never actually murdered anyone. He'd use the clothes line to terrorise his victims so that they'd submit quietly – loop it round their necks with a sliding knot and show them that if they jerked, they'd be choking themselves.

So it turns out that the only real murderer I've come across was a man in New York once who lent me a book by Ortega y Gasset on Western civilisation. I was going to meet him for lunch to give it back when I'd read it, but before that, I heard he'd shot his wife and his six-year-old child before killing himself. He was a manic depressive. I still have the book, because when I tried to give it to one of his colleagues at the museum where he'd worked, he said it would remind him and he didn't want it.

I heard about Johnnie Thompson turning out to be the Sussex Strangler when I went home to Dad's one weekend from London, soon after starting work in the art world – I began at a private dealer, off St James's. Natalia told me, rather solemnly; though he had been identified in the papers, I hadn't recognised him from the blurry press photograph taken at his committal proceedings. And John Thompson is a common name. He had been rushed into the courtroom from the Black Maria to protect him from the enraged crowd that had gathered. For three years every young woman in Sussex and further afield had been terrified, especially students and nurses, as their residences had been his favourite haunts. He'd been nimble too, something of a cat burglar, stealing into third-floor bedrooms up drainpipes. I remembered him up the ladder, how confidently he turned on the rung to pelt us.

We had supper together that night in awe; we felt we had escaped a great danger. He had been there, at the same kitchen table on many occasions, having a cup of tea after the end of a job. He'd asked Natalia for a photo of herself; she'd been embarrassed, but she'd given him one of her wedding photos, in a maroon frame with a gilt rule round the inner edge; he'd taken it out of the frame and folded it, so that Dad didn't show. He said he wanted to keep it in his wallet.

I went to bed that night in the room which had been mine when I was younger and they were first married. I was cold; in the same way as when a friend dies, you feel the chill nip deep inside the bone marrow. I went downstairs to fetch a hot-water bottle, and returned to my room, clutching it to my chest for comfort. When I turned out the light, there was a noise. I turned on the bedside lamp again. No sound. Except that the hot-water bottle seemed to be amplifying my heart thumping. I was imagining things, I told myself, and switched off the light again.

The noise was in the room. A rushing, soft sound, like slippers on a carpet, coming from near the window, swirling closer, then fading again back near the window. I set my chin and reached for the lamp again.

When I could see nothing, I went to my father and Natalia's room. I opened the door a little, and whispered into the darkness Natalia's name. She murmured, she woke,

I was shaking as I apologised to her for waking her up. I think she could hear that I was really scared, because she came to me quickly and together we went back into my room and searched it, with all the lights on. We found the source of the sound, clinging tremblingly to the inside of the curtain of the window opposite my bed. A bat. And the noise – its flight as it sought a way out, whirling round the room with its radar on, so that it never bumped or touched but spun on, filling the air with its soft stealthiness.

We laughed, in relief, and Natalia went downstairs to the garden room and found a pair of gloves and put them on to prise the creature loose. It showed its delicate, light pink mouth as it gasped and simultaneously blinked hard in the glare.

She's much less of a coward than me, and exclaimed, 'Look, it's really exquisite!' Then she threw it out of the window I'd opened, and we saw it unfurl before we lost it in the night.

Bats are streaming from the head of the dreamer in Goya's famous etching, *The Sleep of Reason Produces Monsters*, and I realised that I was imagining things because the news about Johnnie Thompson had shaken me. I'm over that fear now, and he's in a high-security psychiatric prison waiting on the Home Secretary's pleasure. All the same, I seem to remember that Psyche hears her phantom lover come like a wind in the night. He turns out to be god of love,

Eros himself, in that fairy tale, and they have a little girl, eventually, called Pleasure.

Pleasure. Natalia knows about pleasure. I'd like to, as well. I'd open the window to let in a lover with the soft rush of the dark, if I didn't keep noticing things which make me fasten the latch instead.

No One Goes Hungry

I'd been staying at the College Park Inn for a few days while looking for an apartment when I first noticed the little girl and her father. I assumed it was her father, though they bore little resemblance to each other, because he was giving their order to the waitress with a degree of impatience at the child's hesitation over the breakfast menu. I was missing my own children, whom I'd left behind to earn good American money for a semester's work; my wife agreed it was worthwhile and her mother came to the city to help during my absence. So children drew my attention and I could see that this father knew his daughter's mind, even if she did not know it herself, and that is not the way with uncles or family friends on a special outing.

Child isn't the right word: she was a young woman, really, and she had about her a certain fragile dewiness that comes with the first shoots, with blossom in March. My own daughter is older, and uses make-up now that the regime imports cosmetic advertising as part of the free play of market forces, but I remember that phase when she too was like . . . rainwater on buds. Don't mistake me, I'm not envious; as for predatory, don't even think it! Besides, my tastes do not tend in that direction. I was simply concerned for this young woman.

It turned out later that I'd mistaken the cause of his impatience and her indecisiveness. She was trying to calculate the largest amount they could order for the least cost. The pair was already, at that stage, running out of credit, I was soon to learn.

I was in a small university town in the western Allegheny mountains, aiming to take back enough to live on for a year in my own small country, one of the many that have reappeared in the aftermath of the cold war. I began in linguistics, but I turned to software maintenance, which is more often required these days, after I discovered an aptitude: the linkages are not dissimilar and I am concerned with developing them further. An Internet acquaintance suggested my visit to College Park; we have also been working for a while developing a way of transferring actual matter on-line, not only data – there is a difficult, but indeed short step between sending a book and translating by satellite other matter – and even life forms. Not for nothing do we consider the computer's dematerialised output a direct heir of the imp in the bottle or the genie of the lamp. The expressions – computer bug, computer virus – belong in an intermediate zone, increasingly populous, where metaphors materialise as substance. My colleagues and I know that it is only a question of time before we arrive at the capability of moving phenomena in substance, but not in species – a distinction not unlike the old schoolmen's doctrine of transubstantiation, that the bread and wine are changed in substance but not in appearance. I remember from the whispered lessons in religion of those days when the regime in my country did not permit worship. Such prohibitions are no longer, in the days of the Internet, enforceable. Meanwhile, it will not be long before we shall be able to attend meetings at the other end of a cable, be present and take part in conversations as if we were actually present, while our embodied self remains in place at the point of origin, the bread and wine of our apparent being, while our essence lives and has existence in another form, in another place. These are mysteries to us now, but, like electricity, they will begin to clear.

The girl and her father, in a startling manner, were to confirm my explorations of this potentiality.

Such languages as the computer requires are international, so it does not matter that my spoken English is not very fluent. But my awkwardness in speech and the evident difficulty Americans suffer in understanding my accent had the effect of intensifying my solitude, already acute, for College Park Town (that was indeed the name, a sign of the torpor of the inhabitants' imagination) was small. It had a Main Street and a Second and Third Street; its restaurants had such names as The Eatery and The Diner. I felt as if I were coming into another existence as an outline figure in an elementary school reader. The town was pretty enough, with wooden canopies to shade the pavements; flowering trees with pink tassels like cheerleaders' equipment, and a celebrated avenue of huge old elms revealed the college's origins as a centre for agricultural research some hundred and fifty years ago.

I had exhausted the town's possibilities for entertainment within a few days of arrival. Observing people became my only distraction.

The man and his daughter held me in the dining room of the hotel longer than usual: they were out of character in the place and she was too young to be prospecting for her higher education. A certain turbulence arose around them, flustering the college student who was pouring coffee, and exciting alarmed glances from some of the other guests. Her father – her keeper – was a big man, and his domed, large head crumpled up towards the centre of his dewlapped countenance in deep scowling folds; it was formidable and terrible at once.

'Poppa, it *is* coming,' I heard the child say, in a helpless tone, as his whole bulk seemed set to detonate.

By the standards of small-town America, Mr Grindop, for this was his name, was not a big man. Moreover, he was wearing a suit and tie, not the shorts and overlong T-shirt that encase the swaggering bellies and thighs and arms of even larger-sized citizens. As with some tribal chieftains in Polynesia, American power weighs in the scales in kilos – they would say pounds – of flesh.

But she was a slip of a little thing. Not for the first time, I wondered how such a parent could engender a creature who appeared to belong to another species altogether. She was a lanky, narrow-ribbed young girl, of about fourteen, with quick-moving hands and eyes; her hair cut very short showing the slender neck of a child set on straight shoulders, and the delicate chalice of her head and brow.

When their breakfast arrived, he had ordered Eggs Benedict with bacon, sausage, grits and home fries on the side. Then the waitress set before the girl a heap of tomatoes, peppers, onions, mushrooms, oozing with melted cheese from the glistening yellow folds of the 'Build Your Own Omelette' option. When Mr Grindop pushed away his empty plate, he leaned over and took his daughter's. She had hardly touched it. I could feel, from the angle of her back, her shame.

I didn't yet know that he was only at the beginning of his . . . what can we call it? – his condition? Some might psychologise the hunger from which he suffered as the result of infantile trauma. Others, in the past, explained it as the revenge of the gods. Some, in my country, where weary concepts of sin command fresh allegiance under the newly returned monarchy, would think him a man in the grip of sinful appetite: gluttony – gluttony and rage, that, even in America, pigs do not run around, already roasted, with knives stuck into their flanks, whimpering to be carved, nor do pancakes rain down from the sky, nor chocolates open on the stalk.

I was angry, too, and I called for my check, and left the room, walking past their table, and giving her a small smile, as casually as I could in the circumstances, so that I should not add to her mortification by looking on her with obvious pity, let alone disgust, but with enough courteousness to demonstrate that I was on her side.

Even when I'm most concentrated on my work, I find that the thought of someone or something can remain, below the surface of my consciousness, without interruption to its operations; in the same fashion as the .exe and .bat files keep running under open applications, these thoughts and hopes and desires go on whirring, sometimes making themselves felt more insistently and disturbingly – indeed, sometimes crashing the system! But more generally they remain a silent, imperceptible accompaniment. All day after the scene I had witnessed at breakfast, I experienced this parallel consciousness with regard to Mr Grindop and his daughter. I kept seeing them: a student would loom in the computer lab, his girth darkening the ingress as he decided which free terminal was nearest, and I would look up, hopeful for an instant that this Gargantua was my man – and would be bringing his daughter.

Then, when I started downtown for a break, I was still hoping, even expecting, to see them again. But instead I became horribly alert to food, to the omnipresence of eating, of eating in America. Nibbles and snacks and saucers of peppermints and baskets of popcorn seemed to be lying to hand everywhere, beside cash registers and on tables in bars, and an aroma of malt and maple syrup and vanilla pervaded the air, even in pharmacies. Dazzling cabinets of fizzy pop and packets of biscuits and candy stood alluringly in the antechamber of a library or a classroom, and the ice-cream cone presented a kind of template, for plates were made of wafers or batter so that you could eat the dish your food was served on as well. In College Town, every other building was a creamery or a deli or a taco stall or a grill or a sandwich bar or a takeaway: it was like a special vocabulary test that nobody who had never been there could possibly do. And all these different providers of food were vying with one another to push appetising opportunities of some kind. It would be trite to bring up the size of portions.

I also remembered, with a different feeling of recoil, the custom of bringing potluck offerings to class: my students would set trays of jam-filled doughnuts and cinnamon-dusted buns and gleaming Danish pastries with custard and fruit fillings. And then there was the business of the 'doggy bag': for grazing from the fridge in those rumbling intervals of hunger at night.

America, where no one goes hungry.

But Mr Grindop did.

I finally made friends with Lucie, Mr Grindop's daughter. I met her in the corridor of the hotel. I found her there two days later, scavenging for food from the leftovers on room service trays outside the bedroom doors when, sleepless and claustrophobic with hotel living, I decided to go for an early morning swim, hoping that the college athletes wouldn't be there ahead of me.

'He wants to eat,' she said, helplessly, looking up and twisting a strand of her hair, pleading with me not to censure, to pass on without comment.

But I stopped, and I asked her, 'Why?'

She shuddered and clutched the dented aluminium lid from the dish against her chest, and told me this story – it came out in little jagged pieces, like broken china. (She interpolated 'like' every three words, on average, but I will omit most of them.)

'It happened like this, the hunger. He has a business partner and they had a big project and were always together in front of the monitor, hardly talking, sometimes exploding with . . . laughter, like, when things were going on, things were good. It was a database, like they were selling it to people. It involved putting together all kinds of sources, like taking stuff from here and there, some of it should be free anyways, Dad says, for people to take – he's setting it free.'

I took the lid from her gently and steered her by the elbow to the couch opposite the elevators.

'But . . .' She jerked her head down the corridor, towards his room – their room?

'Come,' I said again. 'It does good to talk, get it off your chest, my grandma used to say, and it works.'

I did want to help her. It was lonely in College Park Town and she touched me.

Her father's operations, it became clear, involved accessing services past security.

'I shouldn't be telling, like, a stranger,' she said vaguely.

We were down in the bar by then, she had stopped twisting her hair and her fingers and was folding up the sleeve of her drinking straw into tinier and tinier pleats as she sipped her Cherry Coke Lite through melting ice.

'If it makes you feel better . . .'

'At first he could log on and do stuff on the web and it'd take his mind off the starving feeling, but then it got worse and he went to the doctor for pills to stop it, but they didn't work.' She was frowning, trying to squeeze down on the tears that were starting in her eyes. She still had a child's eyes, dark and reflective and shadowed by weariness.

'It was a virus,' she said. 'But this one jumped from the computer into people. Intra-species.' She worked her face round the remembered term. 'You activate it by doing something you shouldn't.'

Again she bit her lip then took another sip through the straw.

'I shouldn't be telling you all this.' She gave me a little smile – there was a coquettish streak in her, one that my own daughter no longer reserved for me but for boys, boys she met outside the house and wouldn't bring in.

'Dad sold the package for lots of money after that. He was happy he was mellow – but his hungriness got worse.'

She stood up.

'I must go now, he'll need me, he'll need . . . food.' She put her hands over her ears and shook herself all over. 'I have to find another way of helping him.'

'Yes,' I said. To myself I was thinking, This is no life for a young woman, no life for anyone. To Lucie I said aloud, absurdly, as I followed her back to the elevator,

'Keep up your spirits, my dear, keep on truckin', as they say in America.'

I found an apartment two days later, and I lost sight of them for almost a week, and to tell true, though she touched me deeply, I did forget about them as well as I shopped for a few necessities missing from my new quarters – a coffee grinder, for example (in Z— we like small dark shots; we don't drink pints of latte). Almost a week went by before I saw the pair again. It was in the street, by the entrance to the bus station, where I'd gone to check the timetable for New York. College Park Town was inducing severe cabin fever in me.

They'd set up a stall, covered with leaflets, desktop publications inviting new members of the scheme. The database cost a large sum, but you could pay in instalments with the initial stake set at a figure that looked generous terms by comparison. Guarantees were offered.

She was pitching for them, working passers-by with her shy flicker of a smile. The sleeveless shirt she was wearing was cut away to show her midriff – her navel was domed, like a cob nut and she had a small silver stud through its kernel. Her clothing was too light for the weather: the fall was already chilling the air. There was a feverishness about her as she repeated her sales patter. She promised me improved earnings on the market, and my money back if I wasn't satisfied.

Her father nodded at me, approvingly: he didn't recognise me from the hotel. I was a punter. He was spilling over the edges of the folding stool he'd set up; pale moles seemed to have multiplied over his flesh, on his brow, round his neck where the collar of his T-shirt stretched and bit into his skin; it was as if some toxic fuel was snaking through him, pushing up blisters and bubbles of lymph and fat at weak points in the soft slack bag of his huge body. He had one hand holding a large pink carton of something semi-solid, a 'smoothie' of fruit and cream; before him, a paper packet stood on a pile of diskette packs, with its lip crumpled where his massive fingers had probed to extract 'old-fashioned home-bake muffins with chocolate chip'. This arm appeared like a broken limb of some colossus, lying athwart the offer of his latest scam, its swollen digits crowned by nails delineated in dirt, the remains of meals he'd snatched and devoured.

When he began to talk, Mr Grindop reminded me of an accused warlord from my part of old Europe, sitting in a dock refusing to accept guilt.

'Information is power,' he announced. 'Not military might, nor even nuclear capacity. And information is all there, for the taking, if you know where – and – how to look.'

I didn't say that I worked on shields in software systems, precisely against such raids.

He'd find the weak links in the web and break them, then plunder their secrets.

'Scientists are idealists, many of them,' he was saying. 'They put the results of their research out in cyberspace – free. That way, they register their intellectual ownership, because' – and he laughed – 'they don't believe in exclusive patents for knowledge.'

'And you,' I said quietly, 'see this as a business opportunity.'

'Theirs is a spoiling operation,' he continued, facing me with a hard furrow between the fat cushioning his eyes. 'They're removing exchange value from goods and services. It's not high-minded, it's destructive. I don't go along with this stuff about knowledge being free at the point of supply – I've taken out patents on six, seven, eight information clusters out there, with little adjustments, of course.'

I didn't argue with him. My reasons to be there concerned Lucie, after all, not him, except insofar as he impinged on her young life – though impinge isn't the *mot juste* for somebody of his bulk.

I looked at his face and looked away, ashamed. It was like standing on the edge of a lime pit, where everything that's quick is stripped and rendered down to muck, to swill. I was afraid for her, more than I had been before, when I'd thought their way of life merely unsuitable and his paternal authority a misfortune. But now I was alarmed by the madness in his look, that he would stop at nothing in his illness, to calm his appetite.

She was pulling on a jacket. It was loose and baggy with the cuffs hanging unbuttoned over her hands; she plucked at them restlessly. I could tell that she was starving too, but in a very different way from her father.

He looked, covetously, at the dollar bills I unpeeled from

my wallet, and nodded to her, truculently. She obeyed him, moving off.

As long as there was money, he could acquire what he had to eat. What I was beginning to fear was what he would do when their scam didn't work.

I didn't want to become one of those guilty bystanders who tell police afterwards how they had a sense that something was, well, not right but hadn't felt they could interfere. At the same time, I felt I must be imagining things. She wouldn't make much of a meal, but I began to fear for her all the same, though I told myself it was impossible, inconceivable, beyond the bounds of all human conduct.

So she went on hanging there, in the movie-in-my-brain, larger than life in spite of her near mortal delicacy, thin as the spectral image you sometimes see from the freeway, playing in the air on one of those American drive-in movie theatre walls.

The next day I fancied I glimpsed her, leaving a deli with a bag of supplies, turning a corner into a side street, her gait listless, her shoulders clenched. Then, another time, she glided past in a taxi, her lap heaped higher than the window with shapeless supplies, her small face squeezed tight with thought. But I wasn't sure.

The next weekend, I drove out to the mall; the weather was turning really cold, and I needed some waterproofing. I was in Andronico's – as I passed I was enticed by a Special Offer (yes, even I, with my old world cynicism) to turn in to buy a bottle of wine for my supper that night. Then I saw her, Lucie. Then, whirring slowly down another aisle, Mr Grindop. He was in a wheelchair now; it was motorised, and he was purring from one bowing and smiling 'customer service officer' to another as he grazed at the counters, at diced cheeses and little paper cups of seafood prepared in different sauces on toothpicks.

I saw Lucie take a wind-dried duck from the Exotic Foods stall and drop it, not into the trolley she was wheeling but into the knapsack trailing from her elbow. Her father, meanwhile, was exchanging words with the young Oriental woman in French apron and cap at the cheese board across from the counter. It was inevitable. I tried to warn her by looking up sharply at the CCTV eyes scanning the aisles as I greeted her.

'You here, like, shopping too,' she said, with that nervous sweetness that I knew. 'I can tell a lot about a person from their shopping,' she went on. 'Can't you?' She glanced about. 'Where's your trolley?'

I shook my head and held up the bottle of wine. 'This is it. So, what do you make of it?'

She laughed. 'That you're never home, not even for breakfast.'

'What about you? What are you doing here?' I tried to sound meaningful. I wanted to make her danger apparent to her, I wanted to spirit the duck out of her bag back on to the shelves.

But she turned away and made for the tills, and the store detective came up and asked her to step to one side, and open her bag. Lucie looked at him with a thoughtful knotting of her eyebrows, and said, 'Just a minute, let me get my groceries out of the way,' and began tugging at her cart, nodding towards the line in which I was opening my mouth to protest. Then she moved, and I thought she was going to make a run for it. So I pushed past the checkout and found myself at the automatic doors with the detective, calling out to her not to do this, to stop.

The cart was there, with some of the shopping abandoned in it, but not all; she'd taken what else she could carry in the speed of her vanishing. We looked up and down. 'My daughter,' I managed. 'We had a fight . . . I'll make it up . . .' The store detective hauled me back into the store. I didn't know what I was doing, really, when I took responsibility for her. But I did. She had slipped into my consciousness, you see, as frictionlessly as she'd slipped out of the superstore.

'She just disappeared,' he said. 'Wow! How did she like do that? Like vaporise?'

'She lost her mother recently,' I improvised. 'It's upset her a lot.'

He read out a list of some twenty-odd items from a notepad.

'This was all in her backpack, we got it on camera. Plus some stuff from the cart. You going to pay for it?'

I nodded, felt for my credit-card wallet.

'Okay, sir, this time. But next time – if there's a next time, no excuses, no way.'

Mr Grindop was still cruising the aisles in his chair, sampling. I came up behind him and bent to his ear and threatened him with exposure, with corruption of minors, with theft, with charges that would take his daughter away from him. He whirred round to face me and with his rheumy eyes and glistening tongue, whined, 'No, you mustn't, you can't, I'd die without her.'

I wanted to say, as Americans do in their action films, 'You just go ahead and do that.' Instead I said, 'I didn't report you this time. In fact I paid up, for you, for your . . . groceries.'

He was wheedling, 'Thank you, Professor.' Then, with a small flicker of his sunken eyes, he added, 'Why don't you come back with me and we'll talk, we'll talk with her, we'll do something to make me better.'

I was so sickened by him. But I wanted to see Lucie, to see if she was all right.

When I called back at the hotel, the receptionist pointed to the Guest Phone and told me to call Room 502.

It was identical to the one I'd occupied, before I found my apartment, except that debris of leftovers was strewn everywhere and it smelled of ketchup and something rotten and sweetish, like a poacher's game bag. It was a suite, with a connecting door that led to her room. Mr Grindop whirred over to it, knocked, and opened it. I should have realised what he intended, when she didn't emerge at his knock and he ushered me in.

She stood up from the bed, and at the same moment I took in her thin body like a damp fledgling's, the blueness of her limbs under the pale pearl membrane of her skin, with the pathetic purple thong and tasselled brassière, and the CCTV camera up on the wall. This disgraceful encounter, to which my actions had so foolishly led me, was compromising, I could see. My return cache of US currency was to be diminished, in return for feeding Mr Grindop, if I were to continue in my post at the university. But as I began to turn to leave the room, in a kind of deepening sorrow that she was so inextricably wound into her father's schemes, I remembered the scene in Andronico's and the way she had, as the clerk had exclaimed, vaporised.

So I stayed, but I stood by the window, with my back to her, and said, 'Put your clothes back on, Lucie. I am not a man to be frightened by such obvious tricks.'

She made a kind of hey hey sound, like a small ground nesting bird in the shadow of a raptor, and I felt the old profound pity trembling within me. Eventually, the sound shaped itself into a shake of the head and a refusal.

I turned around and pulling the coverlet off the bed, walked towards her,

'Put this on,' I said. 'You are younger than my own daughter.'

I reached her thin, bluish, almost transparent figure and held out the coverlet, like a hat-check clerk holding a coat for a customer.

She was twiddling the absurd tassels hanging from that horrible shiny undergarment, and so I turned my head away as I unfolded the coverlet to put around her. As I swung the cloth, it was something about the air near her that made me aware that she wasn't there.

Even if you don't consciously take the temperature of a situation, it's always warmer near a human body, especially in conditions of heightened tension or danger, as now. But as I opened the hotel bed's orange-brown coverlet to cover her, I understood, yet without fully understanding it, that my eyes were deceiving me.

Mr Grindop, in his wheelchair, occupied the door on to the hotel corridor in the adjoining room; he had a remote control strapped to the arm and he poked it, bringing up a sequence on the television screen opposite the door to the adjoining room, from which I now emerged.

'Don't go telling me you want your money back,' he began. 'Don't say nothing happened just now. Look.'

A sequence began: myself passing into the next door room, Lucie smiling, kneeling on the bed, swinging her tassels, so far as matters had progressed. But then the film continued: I saw myself leaning towards her, putting out my arms, Lucie twisting away with a ghastly flirting glance over her shoulder, a mask from the pornography shelves, then lying down on the bed. I saw myself, enthralled as I stood drinking in her movements, then beginning to tug at my clothes, to lift my legs to reach over towards her.

I was resolved not to lose control.

'What are you doing?' I turned to Grindop, I was whispering. 'Where is she? What have you done with her?'

He sneered at me. 'I haven't put her anywhere. She's just exactly where she wants to be.'

The film of our coupling continued to play, on a loop, and he remained at the door, until the transaction between us was completed. When he'd swiped my card, he paused the film on an image; the indecencies conjured there trembled, repeated again and again. Then at last he whirred out of my way.

'You can go now, Professor, thank you. While I dial Room Service.'

My time in College Park was gradually drawing to a close, and the thought of Lucie tugged at me, as I ran over in my mind the sequence of events: her appearance in the room, her vanishing, her appearance on the CCTV sequence, the scenes in the hotel room, caught on film. I ran it, this new movie-in-my-brain, over and over again, and my anger and my sorrow and my disgust and all the other feelings I had about Lucie were overlaid by a conviction that her father with his illness had somehow found a way to pass matter through space-time. But, Mr Grindop being who he was, consumed by his own appetites, his uses for the discovery, if discovery it was, were limited to pacifying his hunger.

About ten days before I left, I rang the hotel, and asked for him. The woman who answered said there was no one registered in that name. My determination grew stronger, and I asked for the concierge. Perhaps some hesitation in the receptionist's voice had given me an indication there was something to add. The concierge told me.

'Didn't you hear? Mr Grindop passed away.'

'And his daughter?'

'I have no information, sir.'

The local newspaper, which I tracked down in their office on Main Street, had carried the story: upstairs at the hotel, in Room 502, Mr Grindop had finally burst. 'He pigged out – and pegged out,' read the tagline. There were three paragraphs about the software package he was selling, now under investigation. And, at the end, this: 'Mr Grindop is survived by a daughter, Lucie. Though she was involved in her father's business affairs, she is not included in the inquiry, said Officer P—, and is receiving grief counselling.'

Acknowledgments

Around ten years ago, artists and musicians began inviting writers to respond to their images with a story rather than a piece of criticism, and I welcomed this; I've often used pictures as prompts anyway. 'Daughters of the Game' was inspired by a painting by John Dewe Mathews in the show, *Images on Film* (Eagle Gallery, London, 1995) and reprinted in the *Independent on Sunday*; Lino Mannocci asked me to look at his paintings on postcards, mostly views of the sea from Viareggio, and I wrote the first version of 'The Armour of Santo Zenobio' for the catalogue of his exhibition (London and Florence, 1996); it was reprinted, in a different form, in *Maculate Conceptions*, edited by Nick Groom (University of Exeter, 1997). Juan Muñoz, the Spanish sculptor who sadly died last year, at the early age of forty-eight, had the idea of sending a photograph of one of his works to a group of writers, and he picked out for me his 'Ballerina', an almost life-size bronze of a girl on a rocking base, with bells for hands. This inspired 'The Belled Girl Sends a Tape to an Impresario', which appeared in *Silence Please! Stories after the Works of*

Juan Muñoz, ed. Louise Neri (Dublin and Zurich, 1996), and in *Marvels & Tales* (Vol. 12, No. 1, 1998); a special issue of this journal was reprinted as *Angela Carter and the Fairy Tale*, ed. Danielle M. Roemer and Cristina Bacchilega (Wayne State University Press, Detroit, 2001). With the Hoxton New Music Days in mind, the composer John Woolrich and Emma Hill of the Eagle Gallery proposed I respond to John's music; 'Lullaby for an Insomniac Princess' resulted and will now have another life next year, in an artist's book with paintings by Stephen Chambers. Juliet Stevenson read a version of it on Radio 4 in 1999, and this was published in *Mosaic*, ed. Monisha Mukundan (Penguin Books India / The British Council, New Delhi, 1999). The poet, novelist and psychogeographer Iain Sinclair invited me to take part in a show about traces he was putting on at Keggie Carew's invitation (Jago Gallery, London, 1999): I wrote 'Stone Girl' for the exhibition there. Two other stories – 'Canary' and 'Natural Limits' – were written after A. S. Byatt and Carmen Callil, editing different issues of *New Writing*, asked me to submit something (Numbers 6 and 7, Vintage Books / The British Council, London, 1997 and 1998). The remaining stories just happened: of them 'Murderers I Have Known' appeared in a magazine published in Amsterdam by the PEN Center for Writers from Former Yugoslavia (*Erewhon* Vol. II, No. 2, 1995). All have been revised for this volume, and I would like to thank the artists, writers and editors who invited me to write in the first place, Helena Ivins for her help gathering the stories together, my editor Alison Samuel for her support and skill, and the writing group Kindlings for listening to some of my efforts and providing wise and kindly comment.

Marina Warner
Kentish Town, 2002